"What exactly are you doing?"

Piper was fairly sure she leaped several feet into the air. She spun around, careful to stay in front of the offending pot of noodles. "Linc? I thought everyone had gone home."

"Everyone else has," he drawled.

"I was doing the last check on the helicopter."

"Just like you were checking it over before I arrived this morning?"

"You aren't the only one to take their job seriously." She jutted her chin out defiantly.

His eyes narrowed. "Are you sleeping here?"

"Of course not," she blustered. She frowned, but suddenly he was right in front of her and then they were kissing. She had no idea who'd moved first, but she was terribly afraid it was her.

It was more than a shock when he tore his mouth from hers and set her away from him.

"You're eating here, and you're sleeping here," he bit out. "Why?"

"I don't have anywhere to stay," she said eventually.

HIS CINDERELLA HOUSEGUEST

———

CHARLOTTE HAWKES

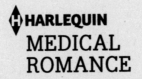

HARLEQUIN

MEDICAL
ROMANCE

HARLEQUIN®
MEDICAL
ROMANCE™

Recycling programs
for this product may
not exist in your area.

ISBN-13: 978-1-335-73735-9

His Cinderella Houseguest

Copyright © 2022 by Charlotte Hawkes

For questions and comments about the quality of this book,
please contact us at CustomerService@Harlequin.com.

Harlequin Enterprises ULC
22 Adelaide St. West, 41st Floor
Toronto, Ontario M5H 4E3, Canada
www.Harlequin.com

Printed in U.S.A.

Born and raised on the Wirral Peninsula in England, **Charlotte Hawkes** is mom to two intrepid boys who love her to play building block games with them and who object loudly to the amount of time she spends on the computer. When she isn't writing—or building with blocks—she is company director for a small Anglo/French construction firm. Charlotte loves to hear from readers, and you can contact her at her website: charlotte-hawkes.com.

Books by Charlotte Hawkes

Harlequin Medical Romance

Billionaire Twin Surgeons

Shock Baby for the Doctor
Forbidden Nights with the Surgeon

Royal Christmas at Seattle General

The Bodyguard's Christmas Proposal

Reunited on the Front Line

Second Chance with His Army Doc
Reawakened by Her Army Major

The Doctor's One Night to Remember
Reunited with His Long-Lost Nurse
Tempted by Her Convenient Husband

Visit the Author Profile page at Harlequin.com.

CHAPTER ONE

THE MUSCULAR MOTORBIKE hugged the bend tightly and skilfully hurtled along the quiet A roads as Dr Lincoln Oakes—Lord Oakes to those who knew his family—raced to work on time.

He was never late. *Never.*

Strictly speaking, he supposed he wasn't late now. The crew weren't due on the air ambulance base until seven o'clock and it was still only six-forty. But that didn't make him feel any less agitated; it was a full ten minutes past the time he usually liked to be in work—always the first one in.

As if timings—not never-ending nightmares of that hellish night in the last war zone he'd been in—were the sole cause of his agitation.

Shifting on his motorbike, Linc accelerated harder and drew down from the sense of satisfaction that slid through him as the sleek machine emitted another throaty roar as it surged smoothly along the road.

As if that would change anything.

As though tearing along these country lanes meant he could somehow outpace the ghosts that haunted him, or silence the voices that whispered their accusations to him in the witching hours.

The nightmares were turning his head into a battle zone so that every time he jerked awake he could practically hear the gunfire, smell the acrid smoke, and feel the scorching Afghanistan sun.

Anniversaries of that terrible night were always painful, but this one—the fifth one—was hitting him harder than usual. No doubt because it had only been a month since the funeral of the old Duke of Stoneywell—the man who had been not only his father but his guide for the first two decades of Linc's life, but who had been more like a stranger these latter fifteen years, and not just because of the cruel disease that was Alzheimer's.

Without warning, memories closed in on Linc, making the scraping inside him all the more intense, and raw. He pushed them forcefully away; the last thing he needed was to be late for his job as an air ambulance doctor and miss a shout. How many more people could he fail to help?

Rolling the throttle as he leaned his bike, Linc powered around another tight bend—as if he could somehow escape his demons. As if he didn't know by now that it was impossible. But if he could just get through the next few days, after that they would grow weaker, and he'd be able to stuff them down for another year.

Finally, the roof of the Helimed hangar pulled into view. The glint of the morning sun off the harsh metal coverings. Down this straight, and a left into the entrance road, and he'd be there—into yet another shift that could mercifully occupy his thoughts for the next twelve hours.

Skidding his rear tyre as he drew to an abrupt halt, Linc threw his leg over the seat and yanked his helmet off as he moved. Another few strides and he was hurrying into the building where the close-knit team relaxed in between shouts, and he waited for familiar sounds to chase his ghosts away; letting them slink off at the door the way they always did when he was around his crew.

But today, instead of everyone being gathered in the kitchen, the usual mouth-watering breakfast cooking smells filling the air, his attention was drawn to the rec room—their recreation space—where there seemed to be something of a meeting going on.

Spinning sharply, he strode down the corridor and slipped into the room alongside Tom, one of the two paramedics on his crew.

'What's the story?' he asked, jerking his head towards the air ambulance charity's regional co-ordinator. 'What's he doing here?'

'You just got here?' Tom craned his neck around in surprise. 'You're always the first one in.'

'First time for everything.' Linc tried to shrug it off, even as he hated to do so. 'So, what's going on?'

'It seems Albert and Jenny were in a car accident on their way home last night.'

'Hell.' Something walloped into Linc, hard and low. 'What happened?'

Albert had been their Helimed crew's pilot for as long as anyone could remember and was like a father figure to the rest of them. They had a standing joke that the older guy had been installed along with the oldest parts of the rec room's ratty furniture.

Even Jenny, Albert's real-life daughter, had started as second paramedic on the team on the very same day that Linc himself had begun, four years ago. So, in a tight crew like this they weren't just colleagues, they were also like family.

'Not sure exactly what happened.' Tom shook his head. 'But apparently it's serious but not life threatening.'

'Well, that's something at least.' Linc blew out a deep breath.

'Yeah. We're just waiting on more news.'

'And that's what the chief came to say?'

'That and the fact that he's managed to get hold of an outside pilot for today's shift.'

'Why an outside pilot?' Linc frowned. 'Echo team's pilot is our go-to standby. What about a second paramedic?'

'We haven't got echo team's pilot—not unless he's turned into one of the hottest females I reckon I've ever seen.'

Linc snorted. 'Playboy Paramedic Tom's on heat again.'

Though to be fair, Tom's flirting always came second when he was a shout. Playboy or not, Tom was a damned good paramedic.

'Yeah, yeah.' The other man laughed now. 'I can't help it if women love me. They love you too, only you're too damned prickly to ever notice. As for our second paramedic, it's Probie.'

Linc eyed the lad across the room. In an air ambulance unit like theirs, they almost always had a trainee with them, whether it was a trainee doctor, or a trainee paramedic, and they almost always got the nickname Probie. This particular lad had been a land ambulance paramedic for years before he'd joined their Helimed crew. Making him up to a full-blown second paramedic to cover Jenny seemed like the good decision.

The new pilot, on the other hand, was a different matter.

'Fair enough re Probie,' Linc muttered. 'But I still don't see why they don't just bring in echo team's pilot. At least we'd all know how this particular crew works.'

'You know that Albert had started to talk to the powers that be about retirement, right?'

'Damn, I knew he was thinking about it,' Linc conceded. 'I didn't realise he'd actually spoken to anyone outside our team, though.'

'Apparently HQ already had feelers out for a new permanent pilot.'

'Yeah, well, they've got big shoes to fill replacing Albert. He was a top-notch RAF pilot with countless missions under his belt.'

'And apparently this new pilot is Army Air Corps. Plus she has over a decade's experience.'

Something slammed into Linc before he had time to think. A memory that punctured his chest and then bounced around, rattling at his ribcage, and evading his attempts to capture it.

'Army Air Corps?' he echoed, more sharply than he'd intended.

'Yeah. HQ were desperate when the call came in about Albert so they ended up phoning the regiment up the road to see if the military could lend us a pilot even for the day.'

'It's about eighty miles away,' Linc pointed out jerkily. 'Hardly *up the road*.'

'You know what I mean.' Tom brushed it off. 'Anyway, from what I can gather, the AAC told HQ that they could lend us a pilot, and that she's even getting ready to leave the military for Civvy Street. Regional have been falling over themselves all morning at the idea of securing her as a permanent replacement for Albert.'

The memory rattled harder in Linc's chest. There was no rational explanation for it, yet it was there all the same.

A feeling.

An image.

Piper.

He hadn't thought of her in years. No, scratch

that—he hadn't *allowed* himself to think of her in years. Which was a slightly different thing.

An Apache pilot within the Army Air Corps, Piper had served on several tours of duty with him—including that last one. Her skill and passion for her career had made her a guardian angel of the skies, and a glorious light illuminating the darkness of that hellhole.

And if it hadn't been for Piper's fast thinking and even faster flying, then those enemy leakers would have slipped the lines and managed to get into the hospital where he and his team had been holed up with the civilian patients. Which would have simply meant more numbers added to the body count that final hellish day.

But more than her skill and dedication to her career, the two of them had grown close on that tour, seeking each other out during downtime, sharing war stories, or simply trying to make sense of the events of a particular day or week.

Not to mention the *almost-kiss* the two of them hadn't quite shared.

If his responsibilities to his brother—the acting Duke of Stoneywell—hadn't left him no choice but to leave his beloved army a matter of weeks later, Linc had often wondered what might have happened between him and Piper.

Linc shoved the memories away, the way he had on those few occasions when she'd sprung, unbidden, to mind over the past few years. Whoever the new female pilot was, it wouldn't be Piper. The woman had always been married to her career above all else—there'd be no way Piper would be leaving the AAC for Civvy Street. She'd always joked that they'd probably have to carry her out of that job in a wooden box.

'Linc?' Tom's voice dragged him back to the present and he forced himself to focus on his colleague.

The last thing he needed was another haunting by his past right now.

'Yeah? Oh, right?' His voice sounded scratchy, but that couldn't be helped. 'Well, I guess an ex-AAC pilot wouldn't be a bad stand-in for the crew.'

'And if Albert's finally ready to enjoy a bit of retirement, then we can't exactly begrudge him that, can we?'

'Right,' Linc grated, his mind still racing despite his attempts to calm it.

It was almost a small mercy when a flurry of movement in the corridor negated the need for him to add more, as the charity's regional co-ordinator bustled cheerfully back in, a figure at his back.

'Okay, team, I'm delighted to introduce you to your new pilot. This is Piper Green.'

Linc's entire world—his entire being—went suddenly, somehow…liquid, and yet granite hard, all at the same time. It was a miracle his diaphragm could even move enough to allow him to keep breathing.

For a moment, he had to wonder if he was seeing things…if she'd been conjured up by the fact that he'd just been thinking about her. And the morning sun shining at her back like some kind of prophetic halo only made it seem all the more as though the image from his head had somehow slid out into the real world.

But slowly, *slowly*, his brain began to process what his eyes were seeing.

'Legs?'

Linc was hardly aware of uttering her name— well, nickname, anyway. He certainly didn't recognise his own voice, and the fact that he hadn't uttered it loudly meant that she oughtn't to have heard him from her position across the room. But he didn't think it was his imagination that she turned her head slowly and she looked straight at him, those familiar, all too expressive rich amber depths seeming to pierce right through him.

The five years fell away in an instant. It might as well have been yesterday that they'd last seen each other. There was no denying that…*thing* that still coursed between them, as powerful, and greedy, and urgent, as it had once been. For several long moments, Linc simply drank her in. As if he were back in that parched, bone-brittle desert, and she were his only source of crystal-clear water. He might have known it couldn't last long.

Abruptly, something followed the attraction; something that was far more potent—and unwelcome—than mere chemistry. It punched through Linc in that split second before he quashed it, and it was all he could do to stay standing in the doorway—affecting a casual air—as he folded his arms across his chest. As though that could somehow protect him from the emotions charging through him.

Attraction. History. But worst of all, *guilt*. For leaving at the end of that last tour without even a word. Because he didn't let people get close and he didn't get attached.

And Piper had threatened to do both.

Dimly, Linc became aware of his crewmate talking, but it was impossible to process anything over the roar in his head.

'Say again?' he murmured.

He wasn't sure he could have dragged his gaze from Piper, even if he'd tried. And by the way she was staring back at him—slightly wide-eyed and just as dazed—he thought perhaps she was finding it just as surreal. But if he didn't get a grip quickly, the entire crew was going to know that something was up and that might lead to questions he wasn't prepared to answer.

Even to himself.

With a concerted effort, Linc forced a more neutral expression onto his face, and lifted his voice to something approaching a normal tone.

'Hello, Piper, it's been a long time. Welcome to Heathston Helimed, otherwise known as Helimed hotel one-niner.'

Linc was here?

Somehow Piper resisted the compulsion to shake her head. As if that could somehow dislodge the apparition that stood in front of her.

'*Doc?* Major Lincoln Oakes?' she heard herself say. Casually. Teasingly. Somehow conveying the impression that she was in total control, when the reality was that her legs thought they might buckle under her at any moment. 'It can't be.'

This was the man who had haunted her across time, and the planet, for the past five years? Even as she eyed him, it felt as though their history was unrolling between them—as rich as any eleventh-century tapestry—for the entire Helimed base to see, if she wasn't careful.

For the better part of six months, on the worst tour of duty she'd ever been on, he'd been her go-to. The person she'd most looked forward to seeing—in the mess hall, in the officers' tent, or even just on the sandy perimeter line that made for a makeshift running track in that godforsaken camp—to offload the events of the day.

In an environment like a theatre of war, bonds could be forged quickly. Tightly. It was entirely possible for a colleague to know and understand you better than your own family. And it had been like that with Linc. They'd somehow...*clicked*.

Until their *almost-kiss* had nearly ruined it all.

They'd agreed it was a mistake—a line they would never again risk crossing—and still, a month later he'd left the armed services altogether, leaving her feeling vulnerable, and foolish.

If she'd known he was part of this crew, she would never have taken the post—emergency or not.

Okay, that wasn't precisely true. But she would surely have been better prepared for the inevitable encounter. A strong pep talk maybe—that reminded her just how she could resist Lincoln Oakes's particular brand of all things male. Thank goodness she'd already changed into the armour of her heavy-duty flight suit.

Not that it seemed to matter. Somehow, she still felt half naked and completely exposed in front of him.

'You two know each other?'

Piper blinked, startled. She turned her attention to the paramedic standing next to Linc, with his practised smile and easy charm. The guy was clearly accustomed to women falling at his feet, and he was certainly good-looking. But she hadn't even noticed him, standing next to Linc. From the instant that Linc had spoken, her entire world had zoomed in on just the two of them—like the narrow shot of one of those photographs she'd taken out in that bleak war zone.

She didn't care to analyse what that said about her. Or her unresolved feelings for a man she hadn't seen in half a decade, and hadn't really expected to ever see again. No matter what little fantasies her subconscious had conjured up sometimes, in the dead of night.

But now wasn't the time to dwell on that. Piper dredged up a bright smile and tried to remember what the guy had even said. Nothing came to mind, and it was a relief when Linc's rich, steady voice answered instead.

'Piper was an Apache pilot back when I served. We did a couple of tours together.'

'Apaches?' The other guy nodded with another practised grin. 'Sweet.'

And Piper couldn't help noticing the way Linc's jaw tightened. Was he remembering the undeniable chemistry that they'd once shared? Even if they'd deemed it too inappropriate for their respective military roles? Or was that purely in her own head?

Even now, as she watched him smooth his chin with his forefinger and thumb, a delicious shiver rippled over her back. How insane was it that she could still recall precisely how it had felt when that calloused thumb had once skated over her cheek to brush away the desert dust that seemed to get into absolutely everything? The way her breath had caught as his head had dipped, ever so slightly, towards hers.

And then the camp's shrill sniper alarm that had ripped them apart.

Piper tried telling herself that it was that particular all too vivid, adrenalin-pumping memory that made her blood pound through her body right now. A physiological reaction to that alarm call, rather than to the man standing right in front of her.

Maybe she would have believed the lie, had regret not still rippled through those nights when the ghosts of that almost-kiss would tiptoe through her dreams. A muted sorrow that the single moment five years ago had been shattered, their one chance gone.

No, she'd certainly never expected to see Linc again. Yet suddenly, here he was. Here *she* was.

It didn't matter how hard the logical, practical side of her brain told her that it was merely coincidence, it didn't silence the low, deep hum inside her. A hum that told her it wasn't just chance—it was something more. Something she didn't dare put a name to, but if she had dared, she might have called it...*fate*.

'So she's a good pilot, then?'

The colleague's question brought her crashing back to reality—to the here and now. She watched as Linc did that thing with his head that wasn't a shrug, precisely, but was just as non-committal. Standard, unreadable Major Lincoln Oakes.

'Yeah, Piper's a good pilot, and what we called army barmy,' he confirmed evenly to his colleague before turning back to her. 'So you can't seriously be thinking of jacking it in and heading to Civvy Street?'

There was something strangely comforting in his words, although his question set off the pounding in her chest again. Though this time for a different reason. He was right, the Army Air Corps had been her life—*flying* had been her life—but the army had its own drum beat, and it was her time to move on from Captain and get her Majority. But a Captain flying helis was appropriate— a Major flying them was not. And you couldn't exactly tell the Army that you didn't want a promotion.

Besides, running a flight-training wing would have taken her further from her mother and brother, for longer. And they both needed her; now as much as ever.

Still, Linc didn't need to know any of this.

'Not thinking of.' She wasn't sure where the nonchalant laugh came from, but at least it sounded a lot more natural than it felt. 'Already done. Paperwork went in three months ago and I'm officially out the door within this next month, hence why they were happy to loan me out to your air ambulance when they got the emergency call this morning.'

'You drove down this morning? It's a ninety-minute drive.'

'One of my colleagues flew me in,' she explained, awkwardly. Though she couldn't have said why.

It was almost a relief when the paramedic inadvertently rescued her.

'Who cares whether she drove, or flew in?' he clucked, making her smile despite everything. 'Allow me to be more welcoming than my colleague here. I'm Tom, Heathston Helimed's most eligible bachelor—August edition. It's great to meet you, Piper.'

There was such an easy likeability to the guy that she couldn't help grinning. At least it was easier than all the sizzling tension between her and Linc.

'Hi, Tom. Nice to meet you.' She grinned, shaking the paramedic's outstretched hand. 'Sorry about your crewmate, Albert. I hope he makes a speedy recovery.'

'We all do,' Tom agreed. 'Though, in the meantime, it looks as though you're the newest member of Helimed hotel one-niner—*Legs*, was it?'

'Old army nicknames,' Linc dismissed smoothly. 'Shared tours of duty. That's it.'

Tom looked greedily from one to the other.

'Nah, there's a story here, right? I can feel it in my bones.'

'Your bones are just going to have to wait, then.'

Piper whirled around as another crewman, who she'd seen manning the air desk in the room across the hall, now stepped through the doorway. 'Nine-nine-nine call just came in; not a lot of info, just that there's a kid on a bike somewhere near Roughston Lake. He's gone over and it sounds like there's an arterial injury; he's bleeding from his groin.'

'Piper,' the regional coordinator followed the crewman. 'I appreciate we haven't finished your briefing yet but...'

'No problem, I'll get the heli started.' Piper nodded grimly, heading rapidly out of the room and to the hangar. At least she'd already prepped the bird earlier that morning, and taken it out to the tarmac.

She didn't need to wait for anyone to tell her that they needed to get up into the air. She could practically hear Linc's voice in her head, reminding her that every second mattered. Here, as much as on the battlefield.

Which was exactly what she needed to also remind her of the other rules they'd had out there, in that war zone. Namely, steering clear of whatever it was that still arced between them. Because the truth was that they would never act on it.

They couldn't.

It wouldn't be professional. Which was why nothing had ever *really* been going to happen whilst they served together, and nothing would happen now. Better to eject all unsolicited thoughts about Lincoln Oakes out of her head, and try instead to reinstate the banter, and the old rapport they'd once shared.

Anything to protect her mother and brother and stop questions about why she'd turned her back on her army career—the career that had always meant so very much to her.

CHAPTER TWO

'THIS IS HELIMED hotel one-niner,' Piper confirmed to the region's air traffic control a few minutes later. 'We have four on board and we're ready for lift; heading for Roughston Lake, just a few minutes up the road.'

None of them were dwelling on the fact that if it was an arterial injury then the kid could bleed out before they even arrived.

A moment later, the radio crackled and her flying permission was granted. Lifting the helicopter into the sky, she circled it around and headed off into the skies.

'Do you know where you're heading?' Linc's voice came over the internal helicopter intercom, from his seat in the cockpit beside her.

As she understood it, he would usually travel in the rear of the craft, being the critical care doctor, and one of the paramedics would sit up front with her as the navigational pilot, but she wasn't surprised he was up here now. Assessing her on this first run. Typical Major Oakes-style. By the easy acceptance of the rest of the crew, they didn't seem to be finding it all that startling, either.

'Yeah, with the barracks just up the road, I've flown around this region for years. Besides, I was going to head for Roughston Lake until more info comes through.'

She saw, rather than heard, Linc's nodded grunt of agreement.

They didn't have to wait long for their update. A couple of minutes later, the air desk crewman's voice came over the system from back at the base.

'Helimed hotel one-niner, this is hotel zero seven, we have an update on the casualty, over.'

'Go ahead, hotel zero seven.' Piper automatically flipped her comms to respond, her years of training kicking in despite the unsettling feeling of having Linc back on the scene.

'Seems the patient was taking part in some unofficial dirt-bike races in the woods to the north side of the lake when a collision occurred. They're quite deep in and the land crew are having trouble reaching them. The patient was propelled approximately six feet up into the air, along with his bike, and when he landed the handlebars of the bike fell onto him. He was bleeding profusely, but the other racers have allegedly managed to staunch it.'

Without even realising what she was doing, Piper cast Linc a look. They both knew that the injury was serious. The patient could bleed out in a matter of minutes, so it was up to them to find a way to get to them. Fast.

'Message received, hotel zero seven,' Linc acknowledged. 'We're about two minutes out but the area to the north is quite densely wooded. Can you get someone to step into a clearing and try to signal to us, over?'

'Roger that, Helimed hotel one-niner. Will ask now. Out.'

'Best landing area?' Piper asked over her headset as the air desk clicked out.

'There are only a couple of possibilities.' Linc's voice was tight, but it was the expression on his face that told her a fuller story.

Evidently, if she wanted to land close then she was going to have to do some pretty nifty flying.

Sure enough, Tom's voice crackled over the headset from his seat in the rear, next to a probationary paramedic lad who had only been introduced to her as Probie.

'No, you can't land on the north side. We've been here before and the main race humps are deep into the woods. It's too dense to land so Albert had to ground us close to the lake and we had to trek in. It takes about ten minutes.'

'The lad likely doesn't have ten minutes,' Linc noted grimly. 'Can you get us any closer, Piper?'

Focussing on the woods, she looked for anything that might work.

'Look for a track or a clearing,' Piper urged, nosing her helicopter forward.

'Like I said, it's too dense and—'

'There's a track at nine o'clock position,' Linc

interrupted Tom's caution as Piper brought the heli around.

'I have visual,' she confirmed, dropping slightly to get a better look. 'It's narrow, and the ground is bumpy.'

'But you can land it?' Linc urged.

Piper took another look. There looked to be a marginally wider section about fifty metres further up. The pylons were still there, but they dipped a little further into the tree line. It wouldn't be the easiest landing...but then again, it wouldn't be the hardest she'd ever managed either.

'I can land it,' she agreed. 'Probie, you're going to have to watch my tail. Tom, check the rotors on the right side. Linc...'

'I've got the left,' he said immediately, reading her thoughts. 'You just focus on the wires and the landing.'

Edging forward, angling her heli as they went, Piper dropped lower. Lower.

'Tail might be a bit low,' Probie's nervous voice suddenly piped up. 'I'm not sure... I can't...'

'Can you go forward another metre?' Linc asked, his calm voice taking over.

Piper eyed the track ahead of her. Another metre forward could be too close on the nose. But perhaps she could land on the hump a little further again, clearing both the nose and tail. She cast a critical eye over the power lines. Further forward would be moving out of the widest part, but she was fairly sure there could be enough room if she angled the heli a little more.

'How are the rotors looking on the left if I move forward about ten metres, Linc?'

He craned his neck for a better view. Tom and Probie were silent, clearly out of their depths. But she could deal with that. She absolutely trusted Linc's assessment anyway.

How unexpectedly easy it was to fall back into being a team with him. As it once was.

'Yeah,' he answered after a moment. 'It'll be tight but there's room.'

'Keep visual.'

'Understood.'

Carefully, she edged forward, constantly reassessing the wires, the rotors, the tail, confident that Linc was doing the same on the left side. And then, finally, they were down safely. Less than eight minutes since the emergency call had first come in.

'Nice flying.'

And it was ridiculous how good the compliment—however gruffly uttered—made her feel. But Linc was straight back onto the task.

'Okay, Probie.' He leapt out of the aircraft and grabbed his bags, with Tom following suit. 'Stay with Piper to help shut the heli down, then bring bloods and additional kit as fast as you can.'

And the next moment he was gone, racing along the track towards the waiting rider. Disappearing over a ridge exactly the way he'd done the last time she'd seen him, five years ago almost to the week.

'All right, fella, I'm Linc. I'm the air ambulance doctor. I'm here to help. Can I get in there, lads?'

Slipping through the cluster of dirt-bike riders—their bikes strewn around the area like machines at an abandoned scrapyard—Linc crouched down next to a couple of lads as they pressed some sort of coat to the fallen rider's wound.

By the lad's pallid countenance and the amount of blood on the ground around him, the injury was going to be severe, but the kid was alive.

'Well done, lads,' he praised. 'You've done a good job here, a really good job. Can you talk us through what happened whilst I take a look at your buddy? What's his name?'

'Kev,' one of them choked out, dazedly wiping his bloodstained hands on his padded trousers. 'He was near the front of the pack when he came off going over the mound. I don't know if he landed on the bike or the bike landed on him, but by the time the rest of us came up the rise, the bike was there, and there was blood, like, pouring out of him. We didn't know what to do except try to stop it somehow.'

'You did really well,' Linc reassured him. 'Did Kev lose consciousness at any time that you know of?'

'Don't think so.' The other lad shook his head wildly. 'Don't know, but he was groaning and crying out by the time we got on scene.'

'Okay, great,' Linc assured again before turning to the kid lying on the ground in front of him. 'Okay, Kev, mate, I'm going to need to take a closer look.'

As Tom slipped the mask over the rider's face to help him breathe, Linc removed the coat and carefully inspected the wound, the young lad's groans getting louder.

'Punctured the femoral,' Linc murmured the confirmation to the paramedic before adopting a deliberately breezy tone as he addressed his patient, all the while packing stuff into the wound to try to staunch the flow. 'You've got good mates here, they've kept you going. I just need to get the bleeding stopped, and then we can give you some pain relief. Yeah, I know that hurts, mate, but you're doing great. Your mates did a really good job.'

More than that, if it hadn't been for the other riders applying pressure, the likelihood was that their friend would have bled to death before the air ambulance crew had arrived.

And even with everything those kids had managed, if it hadn't been for Piper's unparalleled flying skills, then his crew would have had to put down a mile up the track and by the time they'd raced to the scene, it could have already been too late.

Maybe having Piper around didn't need to be so...*unsettling*, after all. She was a great pilot, and hadn't they always agreed that their professional lives came first—above everything else? It was the way they'd managed to keep that distance between them during that last tour, anyway.

So why would that be any different now?

Thrusting the jumble of thoughts out of his mind, Linc focussed on his patient, packing the wound, and applying a tourniquet, all the while talking to the groaning lad. It was a good sign that Kev could answer some of his questions, even through the pain, and it made their job faster. Finally, Linc turned back to his paramedic.

'The kid's going to need a transfusion. Can you get more info out of the group, and find out where Probie is with the other kit?'

At least the aircraft carried some blood and they could give him a transfusion. In the meantime, now that the bleeding was stemmed properly he could offer Kev some pain relief. The kid might not be able to feel his lower leg, but he was clearly in pain.

Linc worked quickly and efficiently on his patient as Probie raced up within moments with the second kit bag. The sooner they could get him to hospital, and to the vascular surgeons whom he needed, the better.

Linc's primary concerns now were about stabilising his patient and dealing with haemorrhagic shock.

'Blood pressure is one-twenty over ninety,' Tom advised him after a moment.

'SATS?'

'Ninety-five.'

Linc nodded, running through a final head-to-toe examination.

'Okay, let's get him onto the scoop.'

Within minutes, the team—assisted by a couple of other riders recruited by Linc—were carrying the kit and the patient as quickly yet smoothly as they could over the undulating terrain, back to the helicopter. Time was still of the essence, of course.

Linc cast another glance at the monitors attached to his patient. The kid was a fighter, that was for sure, alert and responsive so far, and his blood pressure seemed to be holding fairly steady. Now Linc just needed to keep him that way right up to reaching the hospital.

And who better to get them there quickly than Piper?

As if to prove his point, by the time the stretcher reached the landing spot, Piper was out and opening up the door for them to load the patient, slotting into her role and working with them as quickly and harmoniously as if she'd been a part of the crew for decades, rather than not even a day.

As if she fitted.

So maybe he should just get over his own personal feelings and take comfort from the fact that, of all the pilots that Regional could have got to cover Albert's sick leave, Piper was one of the best.

And he'd just have to find some way to live with his own sense of guilt.

'Talk about a baptism of fire,' Tom was gushing as Linc sauntered into the Helimed's rec room, an hour or so later. 'That landing was the most awesome thing I've ever seen. I don't know if even Albert could have made it. And then whipping the heli around that fast for that second shout…? Man, you're one helluva pilot, Piper Green.'

'Thanks.' Piper smiled, but it wasn't the bright, life-loving smile Linc recognised from five years ago.

It was just a little bit dimmer. A little sadder.

'So, you were saying that you flew Apaches,' the paramedic pressed obliviously, the admiration unmistakeable in his tone. 'Aren't there, like, two or three female Apache pilots?'

And it didn't matter how many times Linc told himself that Piper was a crewmate and nothing more, he couldn't stop his gut from tightening at the dark cloud that skittered over her lovely features before she deftly concealed it.

What was she hiding?

'There are only a few of us, yes,' Piper admitted after a moment, before seemingly reluctantly correcting herself. 'A few of *them*.'

Did she miss her Apache? Linc couldn't help wondering. It wouldn't have surprised him. Piper had always seemed committed to her career in the military—surely something had to have happened to make her leave?

And then, in the next thought, he reminded himself it was none of his business. She didn't need anyone nosing into her life any more than he would want anyone looking into his life. Into his secrets.

'I've got paperwork to finish up,' he muttered, making his excuses and leaving the room.

Anything to get away from Piper, and questions about what she'd been up to in the five years since he'd last seen her.

Slamming the door to his room, he sank down in the tattered wingback that he'd salvaged from some skip a couple of years earlier, and propped his feet up on the battered coffee table opposite.

There was no paperwork to finish, he'd already completed that well before he'd headed for the rec room, but perhaps a quick nap might help him to catch up on the last couple of weeks' worth of broken sleep.

It was certainly easier to switch off here, with the lull of noise down the hallway, than it was back in the oppressive silence of his own apartment. Thrusting his hands behind his neck, Linc closed his eyes and tried to nod off.

The sharp rap on the door had him springing to his feet—all the evidence he needed of how wound up he clearly was.

'Yep?'

The door swung open, but he didn't need to see Piper step through to know it was her. Every fibre of his body already told him that.

'Is this a bad time?'

'No,' he ground out. 'It's fine. I was just finishing the case reports.'

She cast a glance at his desk, then at the wingback.

'Trouble sleeping?'

He frowned.

'Not at all.' He might have got away with it, had he left it at that. But curiosity got the better of him. 'What makes you ask?'

She blinked at him, then squared her shoulders. A gesture so Piper-like that he couldn't believe he'd forgotten it. Or her characteristic bluntness.

'I always have trouble sleeping this time of year. The anniversary of that day, you know?'

He folded his arms over his chest before he could stop himself. Even just her words made the ringing louder in his ears. They made the screams that much more real. And they made his guilt that much more unbearable.

'Yes,' he rasped. 'I know.'

She scuffed her boot against the worn carpet, then seemed to get a grip of herself again.

'It was a bad night.'

Which didn't come close to describing just what hell the fifteen-some hours of that firefight had been.

'It was,' he agreed simply.

Another moment of silence stretched, long and taut, between them.

She wrinkled her nose.

'Do you want me to go?'

He opened his mouth to tell her it would be for the best. But the truth was that her leaving was suddenly the last thing he wanted.

'Stay if you want,' he heard himself say carefully instead.

She eyed him for a moment, then nodded.

For a moment, they each edged around the room, yet always keeping a piece of furniture between them. First a chair, then his desk. Eventually, he settled into his office chair whilst she perched on the edge of his couch.

'You look…well, by the way,' he offered, after a moment.

'Thanks.' She raked her hand over her hair, even as it was tied up in its usual tight bun.

But he could remember exactly what it looked like when she released it from the confines of that net. How soft it had felt that one time, beneath his fingers. That pleasantly light, vaguely coconut scent.

Angry with himself for his sudden weakness, he slammed the memories away. And then she started to speak.

'I never feel particularly great at this time of year.' She bit each word out, as though she wasn't even sure she'd intended to say them. 'I find it hard to sleep. Hard to keep my mind straight, you know?'

He did know. All too well. But that sense of guilt was threatening to suffocate him.

'I like my own company a lot of the time,' she continued. 'But just around this week, I find the solitude a little too…'

'Claustrophobic?' he answered, before he even realised he meant to speak.

'Exactly.' She nodded, with evident relief. 'I just like the company. Even if it's inane chatter in the background, it's comforting to hear it there.'

'Maybe you should talk to someone,' he managed. 'Do you still see some of the other guys from that tour?'

'A few.' She shrugged. 'And we used to get together the first couple of years. But, you know how it is, people get posted off here and there, and we end up losing touch. What about you?'

'This place keeps me busy.' He deliberately sidestepped the question.

'Which isn't exactly an answer.' Piper eyed him

ruefully. And when she spoke after another silence, there was a new quiver to her voice.

'I always hoped I'd see you again. To apologise.'

'Apologise?' Linc frowned as he watched her suck in a lungful of air, as she clearly tried to steady herself.

But it didn't make her voice any less shaky. Nor did it clear that glassy look from her eyes.

'For not doing more. I should have caught those leakers before they got to their weapons stash.'

Linc stared at her for a moment, then, before he realised he was even moving, he found himself walking around the desk and crossing the floor, pushing any last obstacles between them out of the way.

Like the spell that only this woman had ever seemed to be able to cast over him.

He didn't know if that made it easier to accept, or harder to. And he had no idea what he'd intended to say to her. But before he could speak, the shrill alarm signalling a new shout blasted through the base.

Habit and training had them both on their feet and lunging for the door handle in an instant but, for a split second, they stopped and looked at each other.

'Perhaps we ought to talk,' he said gruffly, without knowing he'd intended to say anything at all. 'After this shift. And not here.'

Piper stared for a second, then jerked her head into a semblance of a nod.

'To clear the air?'

'In a manner of speaking,' he bit out.

The truth was, he didn't know what he thought it would do. He only knew that Piper was the last person who should feel they owed him any kind of apology, though he had no idea how he was supposed to articulate the guilt racing through his head at that moment.

'Are you heading back to barracks tonight?'

'No.' She shook her head. 'I'm booked into a hotel in town.'

Linc frowned.

'I thought they flew you here in a hurry this morning? You won't have a car.'

'No, but I can get a cab. In two days' time we have a couple of days' downtime, don't we? I'll head back to barracks and pick up my car then, depending on how Albert's doing.'

'Fine.' He gritted his teeth, his mind still galloping away without him. It wasn't the cool, collected self he was accustomed to. 'I've a spare helmet, I'll give you a ride to your hotel tonight, and maybe we can get a drink and talk?'

Amber eyes locked with his.

'I'd like that.' She pulled a face. 'But I don't particularly want to be the topic of gossip around here.'

'No one else needs to know anything,' he assured her. 'In fact, it's better that they don't. It's just one former colleague giving another a ride into town. Nothing more to read into it.'

Was he convincing her, or himself?

'Besides,' he pressed on firmly, 'no one is even likely to see that much. Albert and I were always the last to leave at the end of a shift anyway, by the time he'd put the heli away and I finished any paperwork.'

It was odd, the way he could see the very moment when her last reservation fell away, and she nodded at him.

'That would be…great, then,' she confirmed. 'Thanks.'

And, just for a fraction of a beat, he paused a moment to nod at her, before pulling the door open and racing down the corridor to the air desk whilst she ran to start the heli.

'What have we got, Hugo?'

'A middle-aged female marathon runner has collapsed whilst training. Husband says she usually trains around fifty miles per week. Suspected cardiac arrest.'

'Send the details through,' Linc shouted, hurrying back into the corridor just as his paramedics were dashing past him. 'We'll get air-bound.'

Because, knowing Piper, she was already ahead of them and had called it in to the local air traffic control. Just another reason why she was the perfect fit for this team in Albert's absence.

CHAPTER THREE

THIS IS A MISTAKE, Linc told himself some nine hours later as he sat in the hotel bar opposite the unsettling Piper, and tried not to stare broodingly at the drinks that stood, both still untouched, between them.

He certainly shouldn't have offered her that lift on his motorbike.

His body was still sizzling from the feel of Piper's arms wrapped so tightly around his waist as she'd pressed her body against his back—making him react as if he were a seventeen-year-old kid all over again, taking the devilish Missy Jackson out on his bike the very day he'd passed his test.

Only, to be fair, back then, having his bike had been more of a thrill than the feel of Missy hugging herself to him. The same could most definitely not be said of Piper, right now. He could still feel Piper's warmth, and smell that vague coconut scent of hers that he'd recognised in an instant. Like a long, slow lick down the length of his sex.

Thoughts that had no business invading his mind did so, all the same, whilst the secluded booth and atmospheric lighting weren't helping, either.

'I think perhaps I should leave you to it, after all,' he muttered. 'It must have been a long day for you.'

It was those amber depths that snared him. Keeping him rooted to his seat despite needling him to leave. Before he did something they might both regret.

'I thought you wanted to clear the air?'

He'd thought so too. Now, he wasn't so sure. He couldn't quite fathom what he thought he was doing here with Piper.

Was he here to clear the air? Or had a secret, traitorous part of his dark soul hoped that one night with this woman might finally slake this inconvenient attraction that had never quite abated between them?

Even now, seated across the low table from him in their quiet, tucked-away corner of the room, Piper was captivating. Simple jeans encased her long, elegant legs, which were stretched out in front of her in a way that exposed tantalising flashes of midriff.

His palms itched with the effort of not reaching out to see if her tanned skin was even half as smooth as he remembered it to be. No other woman had ever made him feel so out of control. Not before Piper, and certainly not since.

'Perhaps I should go first,' she rasped suddenly, snagging him back to the present. 'That apology I owe you—'

'You don't owe me any apology.' He cut her off far more abruptly than he'd intended. 'If anyone owes an apology right here, it's me. I let those leakers get out of the hospital. I afforded them the opportunity to get to their weapons cache.'

'And how were you to have stopped them?' she demanded softly. Too softly. It slid under his skin and he couldn't do a thing to stop it. 'You were the one trapped inside that hospital, Linc, trying to save all those women and kids. I was the one safe up in the skies.'

Linc shook his head incredulously. He thought of the surface-to-air missile that had blasted past her cockpit, leaving her Apache reeling in the air. Another metre and she wouldn't be here now.

Whether he'd realised it or not, it was yet another fact that had haunted him the past five years. Yet another reason why he couldn't seem to find peace.

'You can't seriously think you owe me anything,' he growled. 'If you hadn't stayed—if you'd done as ordered and returned to base—all those innocent people would have died. You saved a hundred or so lives that day.'

She eyed him intently. Too intently.

'Is that what your nightmares are about?' she challenged him, in that same soft, all too perceptive tone. 'Some misplaced sense of guilt?'

'It isn't misplaced. You can't have forgotten

how many lives were lost that day. Our guys, and all those innocent civilians besides.'

'Of course I haven't,' Piper choked out. 'You think you're the only one tormented some nights? I wake up hearing those screams, so vividly. Especially at this time of year…around the anniversary. You're not the only one who feels guilty, Linc.'

'What do you have to feel guilty about?' Each word punched its way out of him. The black truth that he hated to recall, let alone voice. 'You stayed, and went on to do more tours, protect more people. You did everything you could. I was the one who quit the military after that tour.'

She didn't answer immediately, watching him, instead. With anyone else, he would have changed the subject instantly—with anybody else, the subject would never have got this far. But he didn't. He simply waited for her to say whatever it was that was clearly racing around her mind.

As though he *needed* to know what she thought of him, after all that had happened.

'I guess, if I'm to be honest, that's the bit I never really understood. I watched you run into burning, bombed-out hospital buildings—quite literally, Patch—and emerge with a woman or a kid over your shoulders. You never seemed afraid of what might happen. In fact, a few times during that last tour, I thought you were almost daring anyone to shoot you. Like you wouldn't have cared if they had.'

Linc couldn't breathe. It was as if all the air had been sucked instantly from his lungs. Her assessment of him was so spot on, and so damning, that he wasn't sure he could even think.

Abruptly, he lifted his tumbler and downed it in one—something he never did. He didn't even taste it. Still, he stood up and walked to the bar, ordered another and returned to Piper.

It had been three years since he'd drunk enough so that his skull hurt, so that he'd forget everything, but tonight, he thought he might just sink back into that old self. It was that, or grab the woman sitting in front of him, and let them both make the mistake that their bodies clearly still wanted to make.

Drinking the memories away seemed like the lesser of the two evils—even if it was the one his body screamed against the most. At least his penthouse was within walking distance of this place so he didn't have to worry about getting caught on his motorbike and dragging the family name into his night of self-indulgence.

'Talk to me, Linc,' Piper pressed, by the looks of it taking herself by surprise as much as him. 'Why did you leave? It wasn't because of us... was it?'

'No, Legs, it wasn't because of us.' He laughed—a low, hollow sound. But still, he wasn't prepared for the admission that dropped, unbidden, from his lips. 'It was because of my father.'

Or, more accurately, the man he'd believed to be his father…right up until that deliberately cruel bombshell from his mother years earlier again.

But Piper certainly didn't need to know that. Any more than she needed to know that the man had been a duke, or that he himself was a lord.

'What happened to your father?' Piper asked, her tone instantly empathetic as she wrinkled her nose, clearly trying to remember things. 'Did something happen to him? I remember you saying that you and he had been incredibly close before you'd left to be a doctor in the army.'

'It was a long time ago since we were close,' Linc ground out, torn.

Half of him—the logical half—wanted to shut the conversation down the way that he would have done any other time, with any other person. But then there was an irrational part of his brain that seemed ready to spill any number of inconvenient truths to Piper, just because she was asking.

The way he never did.

It had to be the lack of sleep. And the alcohol.

He was terribly afraid it was neither. And then, as if to prove a point, his mouth started moving, apparently of its own volition.

'When I got back from that last tour my head was all over the place—just like everyone else who actually made it out of there, I guess,' he added hastily.

'That doesn't lessen the impact on any one of

us, trust me,' she assured him quietly. 'What happened, Linc?'

And even though every practical fibre of his body told him to shut the conversation down, he found himself not only continuing it, but actively answering Piper's question.

'My…father had been fighting Alzheimer's for years. But when I got home that last time, I got a call from my brother, Raf, to say that he'd really gone into decline during my last tour. My brother needed me to come home. The family business needed both of us.'

The family business, in point of fact, being the dukedom of Stoneywell, as well as Oakenfeld Industries—named after their Oakes family name. With their father mentally incapacitated but still alive, the position of CEO of the board hadn't passed automatically to Raf, and with Linc away with the military, it had seemed that various powerful members of the board, whose plans for Oakenfeld definitely didn't align with those of his family, were attempting a coup against Raf taking over as the interim CEO.

Another few points of detail that Linc didn't feel he could share with Piper. He had already blurted out too much.

'Basically, I didn't feel I had much choice but to leave,' he concluded tightly. 'Though, faced with the same set of circumstances, I'd make the same choice all over again. Raf needed me. So did our sister, Sara.'

'And that's what's driven the guilt,' Piper noted quietly. 'You aren't alone, Linc. I promise you. I stayed, but I feel just as guilty. So many buddies who didn't make it out of there because of that one night, yet I did. You did. There doesn't seem to be any rhyme or reason.'

'None,' he echoed, his voice too thick.

'So you put your family first. You had obligations to them. That's nothing to feel guilty about. In fact, it's admirable. And you and your brother managed to resolve things?'

'We did,' Linc confirmed. 'In time.'

Though it had taken a lot of blood, and sweat from them all, and a few private tears from their usually stoic sister.

'And your father is still…'

'He died.' Linc shook his head. 'Last month, in fact.'

'Oh, Linc, I… I'm so sorry.'

'Thank you,' he bit out automatically. Perfunctorily. 'But the truth is that, in many ways, he was gone a decade and a half ago.'

'It doesn't mean you don't feel the loss.'

And there was something so profoundly sad about her in that instance—a shadow that he thought he'd seen only once before, years ago— that reached inside Linc and tugged—implausibly—at his hardened heart. The one he'd thought he'd locked away years ago.

'You sound as though you're speaking from experience,' he rasped out, suddenly finding he wanted to know more about the enigmatic woman sitting across from him.

He wanted to finally hear some of those secrets he'd always felt she'd held so close—the secrets he'd always made himself respect when they had been serving together.

But they weren't serving together any more— working on the same Helimed team wasn't the same, and, anyway, it was temporary. And tonight had been a first in so many ways, not least the fact that he'd told Piper things he'd never voiced to anyone else—not even Raf or Sara.

What was it about Piper that made it so easy for him to talk to her? What was it that made their connection so...real?

Well, whatever it was, he needed to get a grip, Linc decided firmly, or else he might find himself unburdening himself to her with everything.

And nobody wanted that.

'So, *are* you speaking from experience?' Linc asked again, as though Piper hadn't noted the exact moment that he'd started shuttering himself down to her.

She tried not to lament the loss—in some ways,

she was surprised it had taken him so long and that he'd already shared so much with her.

It was more than he'd ever told her back in the army. More than he'd ever told anyone, as far as she was aware. She'd always found him something of a closed book, guarding his personal life as if it was nobody else's business—exactly the way she'd always done.

In a theatre of war, like they'd been in, it had felt like the safest thing to do. *Compartmentalising*, some of the guys called it. It probably explained how they'd kept each other at arm's length despite the attraction that crackled and fizzed inside her every time she was with Linc. Zipping through her body, straight to that ache in her chest. And, if she was going to be absolutely honest, at the apex of her legs.

She'd never been in any doubt that it was something Linc felt too, even if rules and regulations— and their own ranks—had helped them keep things strictly professional, at least for the most part.

But they weren't out there any more. They weren't even in the military any more—or she wouldn't be in a matter of weeks. There was no safety net. Now, here they were, in her hotel bar, with him sharing secrets that she suspected he'd never told anyone else before.

And she found she suddenly wanted to do the same.

It was a terrifying, heady realisation.

'My father died when I was seventeen,' she confessed, before she thought she'd even meant to. 'I found his death…confusing.'

'How so?'

A hundred things rattled through Piper's brain. Though none of them anything she wanted to say—least of all the way he'd died, or the fact that he'd gone from being a kind, loving father and husband to a violent alcoholic, in those final years. That wasn't just her secret, that was her mother's secret, too, and one Piper didn't feel she had a right to share.

'I was conflicted. He was also…ill in the years before he died,' she settled on at last—because, to her mind, alcoholism was a form of illness. At least, thinking that way made it easier to deal with what had happened. 'He hadn't exactly been the greatest father before his death.'

'That must have been hard,' Linc murmured, and she was grateful that he didn't point out how she'd always told everyone in the army that she'd come from a close, loving family.

'It wasn't pleasant,' she admitted. 'Part of me was glad he was gone. Another part of me felt guilty about not feeling sad enough.'

Linc dipped his head, and even though it was just a gesture, she felt as though he really understood. It was strange, how they hadn't seen each other for five years, yet one night had almost restored that closeness they'd once shared.

She'd missed it—*him*—more than she'd realised.

'Is that why you joined the army?' he pressed.

She hesitated. He'd asked her that once before, way back when. She hadn't answered then. She'd been afraid it would lead to more questions that she hadn't been ready to face.

She still wasn't sure she was ready to face them, even now.

'Sort of…it's complicated.'

'That's a cop-out,' he replied. But the faint tug of his lips assured her he wasn't about to press her further on the matter.

She offered a rueful smile of her own.

'My point was simply that I understand how difficult it can be when someone you love dies, even though a part of you feels as though you lost them years ago.'

'Something like that,' he muttered almost to himself, before turning his attention back on her. 'So, why are you leaving? I thought you were a lifer.'

Another question she wasn't ready to answer. Another situation over which she felt she had no control. Her mother and brother needed her. What more was there to it than that?

'Family obligations,' she said eventually. 'Like you said before, I guess.'

'Right.' He raked his hand through his hair

in a gesture that was heart-wrenchingly familiar to her.

'At least you have more hair now.' She made herself tease him instead. 'Not so regulation short.'

It was still short, but thicker somehow, and soft-looking.

Without warning, an X-rated image slipped into her mind, and even as Piper tried to slam it away she found herself shifting in her chair. The air between them as taut as ever, an almost delicious friction sliding between them, as though Linc could read her racy thoughts.

'I didn't mean…' She shifted again, trying to get comfortable. A feat that was impossible when the jostling feeling was coming from within. 'I just—'

'It's fine.' He cut her off in a tone that made it seem as if it was anything but fine.

A tone that was too heavy, and loaded, and full of all the things they always avoided saying.

'Linc…'

She wanted too much, that was her problem. She might have fought it five years ago, but it had been there, all the same. And now, she was here and the lines that they'd drawn were faded, and weak.

And this week, of all weeks, she hated being alone. Hated being trapped with memories of that night.

'What are we doing here, Linc?' she whispered, her throat scratchy and dry.

'We're...talking,' he ground out. 'Just like we used to do.'

And never mind if keeping himself from crossing that short space from his chair, to where Piper sat, cost him far more than it had any right to.

'Just talking?' she pressed, and he thought the naked desire in her tone might be his undoing.

'Just talking.' He barely recognised his own voice. 'Easy, and comfortable, the way it always was.'

'Except it isn't like that, is it?' rasped Piper. 'Things are different. It's...fraught.'

She paused, but he didn't trust himself to answer.

'Or are you going to tell me that I'm reading something into it?' she asked, eventually. 'Are things just simply awkward between us because I'm about the last person you would want to work with?'

'Piper,' he growled.

And he didn't know when he'd closed that gap, or when he'd taken her shoulders in his hands. But he couldn't bring himself to say anything more, and no more than he could bring himself to drop the contact.

He was trapped—in some kind of painfully exquisite limbo.

'Is it the memories of that day?' She swallowed. 'Only we used to get along well, the two of us, and…oh, I don't know.'

And he could have said it was that—the memories. He could have left it at something they both would have accepted. But he couldn't. He had to push that little bit further.

'It isn't the memories of that day,' he rasped.

At least, not entirely.

And he wasn't sure when he'd inched closer to her. Lowered his head a fraction to hers.

He told himself to back away. That he didn't need the ghosts of their attraction spiralling through him on top of everything else. But he couldn't seem to move.

'Linc…' She barely whispered his name, but it was enough. That longing he recalled all too vividly from that night in his tent. The one where he'd almost kissed her, before they'd remembered where they were, and the job they'd each had to do.

But hell, the need to kiss her again, *now*, was burning through him; so brightly that he thought it might sear him from the inside out.

Her mouth was scant millimetres away, and the closer he dipped his head, the more her eyes seemed to flutter closed. And when his lips finally brushed hers, it was like a kind of song that poured through him.

A celebration.

A symphony.

A glorious sound that he'd heard once before, but then had been forced to shut out for good.

And now, he could hear it again. He could revel in it. As her lips moved slickly with his, and her tongue moved to dance with his, it felt to Linc as though he'd been waiting for this for a whole lifetime. Maybe longer.

Hauling her to him, he revelled in the feel of her arms looping around his neck, the feel of her breasts pressed to his chest. He let his hand caress her cheek, indulging in the feel of her silken-soft skin under his fingers, he raked a thumb over her plump, lower lip, feeling her sharp sigh roll through him, right to his sex.

And he wanted more. So much more, that he was beginning to lose all sense of where he was, and what they were supposed to be doing.

It was only the background hub of the rest of the hotel bar that finally pierced through the fog in his brain and yanked him unceremoniously back to reality.

He pulled his head from Piper, and eyed her for a long moment as he struggled to refocus.

'We can't do this,' he managed.

By the expression on her face, she was fighting the same battle.

'No,' she breathed raggedly. 'We can't. This is…a distraction. Nothing more.'

She didn't sound remotely convincing, but he grasped at it all the same.

'A distraction, yes,' he agreed. 'It's the shock of seeing each other again.'

'The stress of the anniversary.' Piper nodded, too quickly. Too fervently.

As if she was trying to make herself believe it.

'It would be a pleasant diversion, but we still have to work together so ultimately it would be unprofessional.'

'Unacceptable,' she offered with a hollow laugh.

The sound echoed everything he felt himself. Desperately, Linc pretended the tightening around his ribcage wasn't so painful. Walking away from her—again—was the right decision, but that didn't mean he had to like it.

'So this never happened?' she whispered.

And it told him all he needed to know, that he hated the sound of it so very much.

'This never happened,' he rasped. 'We go back to normal.'

Whatever their version of normal had ever been.

CHAPTER FOUR

FROM HER VANTAGE point at the top of the hill, Piper peered down into the valley and wondered how the team were faring.

Another shout, this time a road traffic collision involving a car and a pick-up truck allegedly overtaking vehicles when oncoming traffic had appeared around a bend.

From the information patched through by Hugo, the main casualty for the air ambulance was the fifty-year-old male of the oncoming car, who'd had nowhere to go when he'd seen the pick-up hurtling towards him.

The man's wife had been in a more stable condition, and had already been taken to the local hospital by road ambulance, but Piper could see the fire crews working to release the husband from his crushed vehicle.

It looked less than hopeful, but she'd seen Linc perform enough near miracles out in hellish war zones to know that if anybody was going to achieve it, then it was likely to be Linc. However, getting the patient up the hill to her location could well be an issue.

Checking out the scene as best she could without leaving her machine, Piper looked for a suitable site to land in the event that they needed her closer. Her radio crackled but she wasn't about to disturb her team whilst they were working, as long as she could be ready to move once they called for her.

By the looks of the terrain, the most feasible site was going to be the tarmac of the country lane itself, but the trees lining either side weren't going to make it easy.

Still, she was determined to spot a good LZ if it meant shaving a precious few minutes off her team getting their patient to hospital. Minutes that could, as both she and Linc knew from personal experience, save lives.

'Who pinched the last jam doughnut?' Linc demanded in good-natured disgust a couple of days later, as he crossed the rec room to find an empty pastries box. 'Was it you, Legs?'

It hadn't surprised him how well Piper had slotted into the team so easily—years of being an army pilot in a similarly close-knit team meant that she'd slipped seamlessly into the role of He-limed pilot.

However, it had surprised him that the two of them had somehow managed to fall back into their old roles of pretending the chemistry between them didn't exist. As if the other night in the hotel hadn't happened—another *almost-kiss* to add to the one from five years ago.

His libido could do without making a habit of not quite kissing Piper Green—not to mention that insistent thrumming in his soul, whenever she was around.

He ought to be elated it had been so easy to relegate their attraction to the outer limits of his consciousness. So why wasn't he?

Tearing his thoughts back to the present, Linc watched as their air desk operator poured out five steaming mugs from the coffee machine. He reached for one gratefully before turning to face the room to fully take in the sight of three shattered crew members sprawled over the various pieces of battered furniture.

'You snooze, you lose, Patch. You know the rules.'

In the corner, Piper threw her legs over the arm of her raggedy easy chair and licked her fingers unapologetically—not helping his wayward libido one bit. The thrumming in his ribcage shifted decidedly lower.

He fought to ignore that, too.

It was remarkable how a morning of intense shouts—one of the most demanding mornings Linc thought he'd experienced in the four years since he'd been with Helimed—bonded a new team. Even given the circumstances of Albert's absence. And if his libido didn't kick up into overdrive every time he spoke to Piper, Linc thought he might actually start to enjoy having her stand in.

As it was, pretending that he wasn't acutely aware of the damnable woman every time she entered a room, or left the room, or even shifted position in said room, was becoming exhausting.

Almost as exhausting as having to fight off some irrational urge to cross the floor, sweep her into one of the bunk rooms, and do devastatingly naughty things with her in the way he was certain they both should have done years ago.

It took an absurd amount of effort to eject the thoughts—and the deliciously erotic accompanying images—from his brain.

'I wasn't snoozing.' One-handedly, Linc balled up the empty doughnut box and launched it expertly across the room to the rubbish net—an old kids' basketball hoop—above the bin. 'I was restocking the medical supplies after the last shout. It's part of my job, go figure.'

As if that could convince anyone who might be watching closely enough that he wasn't remotely affected by this particular woman's presence.

'Whilst we were in here with the doughnuts.' Piper laughed, and the sound rippled through him far too easily. 'So I refer you to my earlier comment. You snooze, you lose.'

'Isn't there another box in the kitchen?' ventured the probationary paramedic as Piper rolled her eyes comically.

Sexily.

'Ugh, Probie. Don't tell him yet.'

'Thank you, Probie.' Linc forced himself to laugh before striding to the hatch and reaching right across for the other glossy white box.

Anything to occupy his hands. And his mind.

'Muppet,' he heard Hugo say. 'You should have let them squabble it out for a little longer before you reveal that. It's better than a TV soap.'

'Oh. Sorry.'

'You'll learn.' Hugo laughed. 'I reckon you're best off staying out of it where these two are concerned. I've a feeling they're going to be like an old married couple.'

'You two are married?' Probie gaped, eyes wide as Piper spluttered into her coffee. 'Aw, man, how come I didn't realise that before now?'

Linc grinned again, taking advantage of Piper's coughing fit to enlighten the poor kid.

'Yeah, happily married. Ten years now. We've got five kids and Legs is a complete slob. Our house is a tip.'

'You're kidding?' breathed Probie, his eyes flickering from one to the other.

'We are *not* married,' countered Piper, still spluttering. 'I wouldn't go near Patch if he was the last man on earth. And I'm not a slob.'

'Sure you are.' Linc was thoroughly enjoying himself as she narrowed her eyes at him.

And, just for a fraction of a heartbeat, their

gazes held. That split-second memory of the one time when something almost had happened between them. The kiss that still haunted his deepest dreams to this day. And as Piper half lifted her hands, as though she'd been about to brush her fingers over her lips, he knew that she too was thinking of that night.

But then, abruptly, she gave a toss of her head as if to shake the unwanted memory aside, and offered a snort of derision.

'My tent was always tidy, even out in Camp Harton. But anyone would look messy next to neat-freak Patch here. Or so the colonel said. Even the battlefield hospital area seemed that bit more ordered when Linc was around.'

'Wait.' The young paramedic looked from one to the other. 'So, you aren't really married?'

'We aren't really married, Probie,' Linc managed, determined not to let anyone see his internal struggle to regroup.

'But Hugo said…?'

'I simply meant that I reckoned, since they'd served together, that they were going to *act* like an old married couple.' The air desk operator chuckled.

'Is that why he's called Patch?' Probie asked suddenly. 'Because he has OCD and likes a clean patch.'

'Nope.' Swinging around, Piper brushed the

sugary crumbs off her cargo trousers. 'He's called Patch because he used to patch soldiers up.'

'Oh, I get it. And you're called Legs because you flew a helicopter instead of marching?'

'Nope.' Linc snorted. 'She's called Legs because she ran like a gazelle every time the alarms went off. She was always the first to her heli in a shout.'

Although, privately, he could think of other reasons why her nickname was so damned fitting for her.

'Yeah, I get it.' Probie nodded eagerly. 'Patch and Legs.'

'For the record, Probie,' added Hugo kindly, 'I don't recommend you call either of them by those names. I've a feeling those are nicknames the pair of them earned serving together out in some war zone. We didn't earn that right.'

'It's cool.' Piper shrugged, but her smile was overbright.

Linc said nothing. Hugo was right, it would be anything but *cool* if anyone who hadn't been on that tour of duty with them used those nicknames. And by the way Piper was carefully avoiding meeting the new kid's eye, Linc knew she felt the same, however welcoming she was trying to act.

'Oh.' Probie sniffed. ''Cause I was gonna say that I couldn't understand why you were complaining the other day about bridezilla, if you already had a wife.'

'Say again?' Piper's voice cut in a little too quickly, and a little too sharply, at least to Linc's trained ears. 'Patch is getting married?'

As though maybe she was...jealous?

No, not *jealous* exactly, he corrected hastily. But...*something*. It mattered to her more than it ought to. Enough to make something pull tight in him.

He eyed her with amusement.

'My sister is getting married,' he clarified.

'Oh.' She squirmed under his direct stare, but to her credit, she didn't back down. 'Sara? Hmm, she's your younger sister, isn't she?'

'Good memory.' Was it arrogant of him to think it proved how interested she still was in him? 'She keeps trying to pair me off for the wedding.'

'Why?'

It was Piper's characteristic bluntness that made him grin the most.

'Optics,' he lied. 'Long story.'

'Ah.'

It was one simple word, one tiny syllable, but it was loaded with so much meaning, and Linc hated that the very sound of it made it feel as though he'd just pushed her away again.

Then again, wasn't that what he did?

As tightly knit as he liked to think the crew

was, he didn't want to share his biggest secrets with them any more than he'd wanted to share them with his buddies back in the army. The men and women in whom he entrusted his life.

He found he couldn't tear his eyes from Piper's as they watched each other without saying another word. If there was ever anyone he would trust with his secrets, then it would probably be this woman.

But not the fact that he was a lord. Or, more to the point, that he wasn't really a lord at all; at least, not by blood—his mother had made that clear, in her own gleefully cruel way. And perhaps it was that which hurt the most. He'd not only lost the decent, moral old duke as his 'father', but the man had also been his compass. And his anchor. Without the duke claiming him as his son, by blood or not, was he really part of the Oakes family anymore?

And Raf and Sara could claim that it didn't matter to them one bit, and that he was their brother no matter what—but he didn't feel the same. He felt like more of an imposter than ever. Was it any wonder he'd joined the army the week his mother had so gleefully dropped her bombshell on the family—in all its brazen ugliness?

And was it any wonder that even now, over a decade later, he still couldn't bring himself to go...*home*?

'So just take someone with you to keep your sister happy, if it's just optics,' Probie interjected suddenly, causing Piper to finally break eye contact and look at the young lad.

Linc felt the loss far too acutely.

'He can't do that,' Tom scoffed. 'You don't take a casual date to a wedding and not expect them to read too much into it.'

'Humble as ever, Tom?' Hugo laughed, as he prepared to head back out to man the phones.

'You can mock, but you know I'm right. Linc knows it, too.' The paramedic grinned, calling after him. 'That's why he keeps refusing dates, even if it risks incurring the wrath of a kid sister. Which, trust me, isn't something you want to take lightly.'

'You have to have some female friends who don't want to sleep with you, don't you?' Probie turned to Linc.

'Men and women can't be platonic friends,' countered Tom before Linc could answer. 'Not really. At least one of them wants more. Possibly both.'

'I'm sure they can.' Probie frowned. 'Look at Linc and Piper.'

And suddenly, both pairs of eyes swivelled to consider the pair speculatively, and Linc didn't need to see Piper's reaction to know that she would be tensing up.

'Well, they're just odd,' Tom snorted.

'I know,' the young Probie exhaled abruptly. 'Since you're just good friends, maybe you ought to go to the wedding together.'

'I think not,' Piper objected, her voice tight.

And even though the logical part of Linc agreed, it didn't stop another part of him—a decidedly more primitive part—from wishing that maybe that could have been an option.

'Probie, I'm looking to convince my sister to stop setting me up with dates, not encourage her. All Piper and I do is quibble.'

'Yeah, like an old married couple.' Probie frowned, clearly not following. 'Just like Hugo said.'

'No,' Piper managed, just as the air desk jockey sauntered back in.

'Forgot my favourite pen.' Hugo paused mid-reach. 'Wait, what did I say before?'

Before Linc could change the subject, Probie had set it all out. But that didn't explain why Linc paused long enough for his old crewmate to answer, instead of shutting it down there and then.

'Might be a plan,' Hugo offered thoughtfully, before grabbing his pen and hurrying back out.

'No,' Piper repeated. *Stiffly,* Linc thought.

'I mean, you want your sister to back right off, don't you?' the crewman continued. 'And you two *do* act like you've got that something-something going on.'

'We most certainly do not.'

'Maybe not consciously.' Probie shrugged, refusing to back down. 'But it's there, all the same.'

'We've worked together before,' Piper repeated. 'Nothing more.'

And even though he knew the truth, Linc found he didn't want to actually hear her denying there had ever been anything between them.

'Enough, guys.' He thumped a coin onto the worktop as a distraction. 'Pool tournament. Who's taking me on first? Only ten pence a wager.'

'No chance. I lost a fiver to you last week, and we were only betting ten pence then,' Hugo scoffed. 'Besides, I have to get back to the phones.'

'I'll give you a game.' Tom stood with a dramatic sigh. 'If only to shut the pair of you up.'

'Suits me.' Throwing the rest of his coffee down his neck and snagging a second doughnut, Linc strode over to the pool table. Racking the balls, he shook his head as though to empty it of thoughts of Piper, and picked up a coin. He definitely needed the distraction.

'Call it,' he told Tom.

'Heads.'

Linc dutifully tossed the coin up and caught it.

'Heads it is. Your break.'

'No one's break, sorry, guys.' The door swung

back open as Hugo hurried in. 'A man's fallen off a ladder whilst trimming a hedge. The electric trimmers have made a partial cut through his upper arm. He's conscious but losing a fair amount of blood.'

CHAPTER FIVE

LINC THRUST OPEN the door of the heli HQ with a sharp kick; the darned thing was sticking again. He made a mental note to repair it at some point in the day, but deep down he knew his sour mood was more to do with the text he'd just received than the door itself.

What was it about his usually fair-minded kid sister that was really pushing his buttons these days? That mile-wide obstinate streak that both amused and infuriated him, though not in equal measure. If he weren't so fond of her, he might have warned her fiancé that Sara was turning into the ultimate bridezilla, and to run for the proverbial hills.

But, for all her faults, he loved his sister to distraction. And his older brother for that matter. And if they were more concerned than he himself was with matters of appearance, and stature, then they were entitled to be. All he'd ever wanted in life was to be in the army, and to be a doctor, and he'd done both.

Ranulph—Raf—had been the one lumbered with the responsibility of primogeniture, as well as all the crushing responsibilities of their father whilst the old duke had been losing his mind to the cruel disease that was Alzheimer's.

Even Sara had played her part as the obedient daughter of a duke and duchess—despite the way their mother had undermined her own daughter, and scorned Sara's every choice her entire life. All because their mother had been jealous of her daughter's youth, and sharp intellect.

And none of that even came close to the horribly cruel bombshell their mother had dropped on Linc himself—from practically her death bed, as if she couldn't have been more dramatic. Finding out that his father was not the loving, kind-but-firm duke, but some playboy jockey who was as notorious for his women as he was for his racing wins, hadn't been the most grounding moment of Linc's life.

It had sent him hurtling from the family seat at Stoneywell for a start, joining the army and throwing himself into tours of duty as if he didn't care if he lived or died.

Back then, he *hadn't* cared.

But things were different now. His life felt more stable in the air ambulance. Still, returning to Oakenfeld for his sister's wedding wasn't something he was looking forward to.

Linc drew in a deep breath. Being the second male heir—if he could legitimately call himself that—unquestionably had its advantages, like ditching his title as Lord Lincoln Oakes, for a start. No one here knew who he really was, just as no one in the military ever had.

Not even Piper.

He was so caught up in his thoughts that the sound of a thump in the rec room caught him off guard.

'Who's there?' he barked out instantly, dropping his bag where he stood and striding down the hall, fists at the ready. 'You'd better give yourself up. I'll give you one chance.'

'Linc?'

The familiar, feminine voice punched straight through Linc. He lowered his fists and turned to retrieve his bag, and to catch his breath. It was one thing to act normally around Piper when the rest of the crew were there as a safety net...but the knowledge that it was just the two of them here now made things shift. Even the air seemed to grow thicker.

He pushed the thought away and strode into the room, frowning.

'You're here early. How did you get in? The door was still sticking when I unlocked it just now.'

'I came through the hangar.' She shrugged—slightly awkwardly, he thought. Or was that just his imagination? 'I wanted to just check on the heli. So, are you putting the coffee machine on?'

He eyed her briefly, but whatever he thought he'd seen was gone. It was definitely his imagination. He needed to get a grip. Piper had a way of slipping all too easily under his skin. He gritted his teeth and held up the shopping bag.

'I picked up a few ingredients from the local store on the way in.'

'Breakfast?'

And again, he wondered if he was reading things that weren't there when he thought that she perked up a little too much at the idea of food. As if she hadn't eaten recently... He knew the signs from the army—those lads who hadn't had a decent meal for days.

'Next time, it's your turn,' he said with a laugh, even as he watched her closely.

'Of course.' She dipped her head but though she did a good job of disguising it, there was something she was hiding.

'You want to start the mushrooms if I start the bacon?'

'Actually, I can't really...cook.' She wrinkled her nose.

'I didn't know that.' He eyed her in surprise. 'Then no time like the present to learn.'

And, under the threat of another wave of that thing he kept pretending didn't exist between them, Linc ducked into the kitchen just as there was another slam against the wall, signalling the arrival of more of their crew arriving early.

He really needed to remember to sort that door

out, too. Something about Piper's appearance this morning still bugged him.

'We've got an eighteen-year-old who has taken a tumble from height unknown at one of the water-falls near Heathston Heights. He's responsive and breathing, but nothing else known for now. We need to get airborne now,' Linc declared, reaching for his helmet along with the rest of his team. 'We can be on our way to the grid until the exact location details come through.'

Racing out onto the tarmac, he wasn't surprised to see Piper already in the heli and starting her up.

'Strong winds today, guys,' Piper announced as she prepped to get the all-clear from the region's air traffic control. 'Good chance we'll be taking off sideways, so just keep alert for me, okay?'

Waiting long enough to ensure she was airborne and happy, Linc patched through to their HQ's air desk.

'Helimed hotel zero seven, any updates, over?'

'Negative, Helimed hotel one-niner, there are no land crews on scene yet, and the initial caller doesn't have much info, over.'

'We're going to need a better location,' Tom grumbled over the headset. 'Or we aren't going to know where to head to.'

'I could take a pass over the most popular wa-terfalls,' Piper suggested.

'Nothing to lose,' Linc agreed. 'I take it the

original caller is a kid who doesn't know which one they're at? Time's trauma and all that, so has to be worth a try.'

He peered out of the window as Piper dutifully took her first pass over.

'Anyone got visual?' she asked.

'Nothing yet,' Hugo denied.

'Nor here,' noted Linc. 'Wait, about two o'clock? Looks like something down there.'

Piper duly nosed the heli in the direction.

'Yeah, that looks like it. Nice spot.'

'A couple of kids are waving us down,' Tom added.

'There are power lines running just up from the river,' Piper noted grimly. 'But I can land in that field to the other side. Looks like a low wall for you to hop over, then a bit of a sprint, but nothing more.'

'Good call,' Linc agreed as Piper was already circling the heli around.

Quickly, smoothly, she landed it.

'Clear to go,' she confirmed as Linc and his two paramedics grabbed their gear and started moving.

It was a good call by Piper to try the pass over, Linc considered. He really ought to tell her that when they got back to base.

'All right, lads.' He turned his attention to the kids as they moved to greet the crew. 'I take it this is Bobbi? Can you tell me what happened, son?'

Squatting down next to the casualty, Linc began his preliminary observations. Although the lad was moving and making sound in response to Linc's questions, he wasn't making coherent replies.

It was going to be down to the kid's friends to piece together what they'd seen.

'He was climbing on that ridge.'

'No, he wasn't, he hadn't reached that ridge.'

'Wait, which ridge are we talking about?

Quickly, methodically, Linc worked with the group, until the land ambulance crew arrived on foot—their vehicle stuck a few hundred metres away in the car park.

'This is Bobbi, seventeen. About twenty-five minutes ago he took a tumble whilst climbing around the waterfall. He lost his grip and fell around twelve feet onto these jagged rocks down here.

'According to one of his mates, Bobbi was unconscious for around a minute, but he was awake and responsive by the time we arrived. He cites general pain around his lower back, towards his right-hand side, and some pins and needles in his right hand. Suspect spinal injuries, possibly T-Twelve fracture, and ideally I want to evacuate with the assistance of mountain rescue, using an inflatable mattress scoop. Bobbi's initially had morphine, but is still complaining of significant pain. We're about to administer ketamine.'

'You got here fast.' One of the land crew para-medics smiled grimly as she cast her eye over Linc's team. 'We couldn't even be sure which waterfall it was.'

'Yeah, it's definitely not easily accessible by road. You did well to get here,' Linc noted. 'We were lucky we got in scene within ten minutes of the call. Our pilot took a fly-by, and we happened to spot him.'

Linc thought of Piper and was surprised at the sensation that punched through him.

'You're taking him back with you guys?' the paramedic surmised.

Linc nodded at her.

'Affirmative. Once we get him on the scoop and into the heli, we'll alert the hospital that we're a few minutes out, and they can have a spinal team on standby. The sooner we get him into their hands, the better chance they've got of mending his broken back. But getting him out of here smoothly is going to be the biggest hurdle.'

The paramedic nodded. 'Should be easier with the six of us. You just tell us where you want us, and we'll do it.'

'That's the idea,' Linc agreed, returning to his patient for the last checks. 'Right, let's get things moving.'

Piper took her time last parading the heli, giving everyone time to leave. Almost getting caught by

Linc that morning had been too close; she needed to find somewhere else to stay. Time for another Internet search tonight.

If it hadn't been for Linc, she might have confided in the rest of crew hoping that one of them might know somewhere. But she didn't want to look weak...vulnerable in front of Linc. She wanted him to be as impressed with her as a Helimed pilot as he had been when she'd been an Apache pilot.

And it didn't matter how much she pretended not to know the reason for her pride, she was terribly afraid she knew precisely why it mattered to her.

Despite her bravado that it would be easy to set their attraction aside again, it was still there, sizzling between them. Only this time, now that they didn't have the rules and regulations of the army to shore up their defences, the pull was stronger than ever, and she had no idea how to snuff it out. She wasn't sure she even wanted to.

But she had to—there was nothing else for it.

Finally thinking she'd waited long enough, Piper poked her head through the door that connected the hangar with the crew area.

Blissful silence, and dark but for a small light someone had left on in one of the side rooms, spilling enough warm light into the corridor that she wouldn't stub her toe in the darkness, the way that she had done the night before.

Padding quietly down the hall, she slipped into the kitchen and flicked the radio on—the place was too deadly silent otherwise. Then she pulled the pot of ready-to-boil noodles from her bag. Hardly the most nourishing dinner, but it would have to do. It was better than the last couple of nights anyway, when she hadn't had anything. Reaching out, she flipped the switch on the boiling water tap.

'What exactly are you doing?'

Piper was fairly sure she leapt several feet into the air. She spun around, careful to stay in front of the offending pot of noodles, and her hand pressed to her chest as though that could somehow slow her racing heart.

Worse, she wasn't entirely sure it was purely down to the shock.

'Linc? I thought everyone had gone home.'

'Everyone else has,' he drawled. 'I had the last case report to complete. What's your excuse?'

She should have realised he was still here when she saw that light on down the hall.

'I was last parading the heli.'

Not entirely untrue, though she wasn't surprised when his eyebrows twitched sceptically.

'Just like you were checking it over before I arrived this morning?'

'You aren't the only one to take their job seriously.' She jutted her chin out defiantly.

His eyes narrowed.

'Are you sleeping here?'

'Of course not,' she blustered.

'You can't stay here overnight, Piper. This place isn't insured for that.'

'Good job I'm not, then.' She hadn't realised that. Oh, Lord, what was she to do now? Well, whatever it was, there was no need for Linc to know her predicament. 'Like I said, I was last parading the heli. Now I'm leaving.'

He leaned slightly to the side.

'So what are you trying to hide?'

'Not sure I'm following?'

'You've never been a great liar, Legs.'

Funny, but coming from Linc it sounded more like a criticism than a compliment. She frowned but suddenly, he was right in front of her, reaching around her for the packet. But she couldn't breathe, she certainly couldn't think. But then they were kissing, and she had no idea who had moved first but she was terribly afraid it had been her.

And he tasted every bit as magic as he had the last time. Every bit as addictive. Every bit as thrilling.

It was more than a shock when he tore his mouth from hers and set her away from him.

'Is this your idea of distracting me?' he growled. 'I must say, it's quite effective, you almost had me. Almost.'

She could admit that it wasn't a distraction at

all, and that the kiss had caught her off guard just as it had done with him.

Somehow, she didn't think Linc would believe her.

'Can't blame a girl for trying,' she made herself quip instead.

But it only earned her a narrowed gaze.

'You're eating here, and you're sleeping here,' he bit out. 'Why? What happened to the hotel?'

Piper dug her fingernails into her palm, silently praying for one last distraction to save her from having to admit her failings to Lincoln Oakes, of all people.

'Turns out it was just for those first few days,' she ground out eventually, 'because of the lack of notice. But once they flew me back to barracks for those couple of days' downtime, they expected me to drive down from there.'

'Every day?' he scoffed. 'It's a one-hundred-and-sixty-mile round trip.'

'It's just over an hour each way on the motorway at that time of day.' She shrugged. 'Plenty of people have to do that kind of commute in the non-army world, so I understand.'

'That's ridiculous. You couldn't just stay in the hotel?'

'Did you see the rates of that place?' She forced a laugh, hating the way he was looking at her.

As if she couldn't organise herself.

Or perhaps she was just projecting.

'Somewhere else, then?' he demanded. 'It might not be the biggest town but there are at least a couple of other places I can think of that are still decent.'

'I tried them both,' she admitted. 'Apparently there's some kind of expo going on at the moment and they're both booked out. So are the affordable but decent places further afield.'

'Oh, right.' He thought for a moment. 'Local B & Bs? There are some good ones.'

'Again, booked out, or astronomically priced.'

'There have to be some inexpensive but decent places a little further afield.'

'Only if I go about an hour out, and if I'm doing that then I might as well drive back to barracks. Otherwise, just whilst the expo is on, they're all outside my budget.'

'Your budget? You're a pilot, you can't exactly be hard up for cash.'

Piper fought down a rumble of emotion. Frustration, guilt, and a couple of others that she didn't care to admit.

'The Air Corps don't exactly pay commercial pilot rates. You know that.'

'Still, it's good pay.'

It was, she had to admit that. Reluctantly, Piper nodded.

'Yeah, okay, it's good enough. But it…isn't all mine.'

He narrowed his eyes at her again.

'You send it home, don't you? To your mother? That's why you joined the army when your father died, so that you could look after her?'

How could he possibly read her so easily? She hated it.

And, at the same time, it was something of a relief.

'My brother was a baby at the time,' she blurted out. 'Mum couldn't possibly cover the mortgage, and the household bills, and the cost of a baby on her own, though she'd always worked.'

'I'm not criticising her, Piper,' Linc said quietly. 'Or you.'

She swallowed. No, he hadn't been criticising anyone. And yet she'd taken it as such all the same—which probably revealed a good deal too much about her more than it did about Linc.

'Right. I know that.'

His expression shifted.

'Your brother was about seven when we last served together, right? He'd be about twelve now?'

'Yes, twelve,' she confirmed, marvelling that he'd remembered such a small detail. 'He's at secondary school.'

'And your mum doesn't work?'

'She does,' Piper countered. 'She took a job years ago as a dinner lady in his old primary school so that she could be there for him before and after school, but it doesn't pay that much and there's no work in the holidays.'

If it weren't for the fact that they needed to protect the young kid from the truth about his dad's death for as long as possible, maybe her mother could have got a better job and paid for afterschool care. He might only have been a baby when his father had attacked their mother, but who knew what a baby remembered, or later tried to process?

Little wonder that her mother had always wanted to be there for her brother, to make sure he stayed on the right path, and didn't fall in with a poor crowd. The kid was completely innocent and he deserved a normal childhood—and that was what she and her mother had always tried to give him.

Besides, none of that was what took the bulk of her money. But there was absolutely no way that she was going to tell the former Major Lincoln Oakes that in those final months before his death, her father had managed to rack up over-six-figure debt—borrowing more and more each month from a loan shark, just so that he didn't have to admit to anyone that he'd lost his job and couldn't get another one.

She and her mother had been paying him back for over a decade now, and they were almost clear. Almost free. She could practically taste it.

The moment they were released from that dark cloud would be the moment her entire family could finally start afresh.

But every penny she had to pay for some overpriced hotel was a penny they didn't have for the debt collectors. And that was something she couldn't just accept.

'So you're sleeping here because the journey back to barracks is ridiculously long, and you can't afford a hotel,' he summarised.

Her cheeks burned hotter, but what other option was there than to tell the truth? It wasn't as though she could bluff it—he was too sharp to believe any excuses. She splayed her hands out in front of her.

'Only because prices are high whilst this conference is on. I can't eat into what little they have. My brother's a nearly teenager, and aside from the household bills, there are all kinds of school bills now. Uniform, sports kit, field trips. Not to mention the fact that, as a boy, he could easily eat us out of house and home. He eats more than I've ever eaten—by a mile.'

'Yeah.' Linc grinned abruptly. 'I remember what my brother and I were like at that age. Still are now, to be fair. We'd inhale in one day what Sara would have eaten in a week. I remember after one full-on rugby tournament, we came home and ate a box of cereal each, and each with a litre of milk. Then a roast chicken and a loaf of bread between the two of us. Then we started on the cake that the cook had been baking for our father's birthday.'

'You had a cook?' Piper's eyebrows shot up to her hairline, and Linc could have kicked himself.

'My mother was terrible in the kitchen,' he covered as smoothly as he could.

It wasn't a complete lie, but it wasn't exactly the truth, either. Oakenfeld Hall had three cooks—the formidable Mrs Marlston, and her two very capable assistant cooks. But the woman had been more of a mother figure to him and to Raf, especially, than their own mother ever had.

Still, Linc kept all that information firmly to himself.

'So what are you going to do now you're leaving the Air Corps?'

'Hopefully I can get a steady gig. Otherwise I'll be a freelance pilot.'

'Meaning if you don't fly then you don't earn,' he noted.

She didn't answer.

'So are you going for Albert's job permanently? You know he's leaving, don't you?'

Linc wasn't sure what he thought about that. The idea of Piper being around permanently wasn't exactly an unpleasant one—far from it. But it would mean that those lines they'd drawn would have to stay in place for good.

Which, he told himself firmly, was absolutely fine by him.

'Actually, I was going for the position of pilot

for the Helimed across the border in the county over.'

'Which one?' he asked, curious despite himself.

She wrinkled her nose at him, as though weighing up whether to answer. It was almost comical. *Almost.*

'West Nessleton Helimed,' she admitted at last. 'It's closer to my mum, and my brother. This temporary placement here kind of fell into my lap. A good hearts and minds role between the AAC and the community, plus it's hardly worth sending me on a training exercise when I'm leaving.'

'And you still need to keep your flying hours up,' Linc realised. 'I fully empathise, truly. But you can't stay here, Piper. Like I said, the insurance simply doesn't cover it and I can't risk this entire base just for one person. Even for you.'

'I know.' She nodded furiously. 'I'll pack my things.'

There was a beat of hesitation.

'Where will you go?'

She squeezed her eyes closed, trying not to think of her mother or her brother. Or the fact that the boiler still needed replacing before winter set in. And of course the newer models meant that it couldn't be swapped like for like, so it would need to be sited somewhere else in the house; which meant floors lifted, new piping laid, and ceilings torn down.

It never seemed to be an easy job, and it always seemed to cost far more than it should.

Carefully, determinedly, she schooled her features so that none of this showed, and instead shot Linc her breeziest smile.

'Like you said, there are some inexpensive B & Bs a little further afield. I'll try them.'

For all his sternness, he looked back at her with concern.

'And your mother?'

'She'll understand.'

And she would. Her mother was always worrying whether she could afford to be sending them so much, as well as paying the mortgage, and most of the bills. It was one of the main reasons why Piper wished she didn't have to worry her at all.

Hastily, she began stuffing all her belongings back into her rucksack. Maybe she could sleep in her car instead. At least that way, she wouldn't have to let her family down. Shrugging her leather jacket on and throwing her bag over her shoulder, Piper headed out to look for Linc.

'Okay, I'm going.' She ducked her head around the door to the office, but he wasn't there.

He probably didn't want to hear anything more from her tonight anyway. She'd be better slipping out quietly, and in the morning they didn't have to discuss it at all.

She was halfway along the corridor when Linc appeared at the door of the kitchen, her noodles dinner in his hand and a distinctly unimpressed expression tugging at his features.

'Are you forgetting something? This was what you were going to eat?'

'Oh, thanks,' she muttered, not bothering to answer the question itself—what would be the point?

She stretched out her hand to take it, but he dropped it unceremoniously in the bin beside him.

'You aren't serious? You can't live on that.'

'Don't...' Piper gaped at the bin in dismay. 'That's all I've got. And I don't live on it. You made a full breakfast this morning, for a start.'

She hesitated, torn between needing the unopened pot, and not wanted to let him see her take it out of the bin. He skewered her with a look.

'You aren't honestly debating whether or not to go dumpster-diving, are you?'

Heat bloomed in her cheeks anew.

'Of course not.'

'And you're still a bad liar.'

'Fine.' She snorted. 'But it's hardly a dumpster. It's the kitchen bin, and I know for a fact that it was cleaned out at the end of the shift so there'll be nothing in there but my unopened pot.'

'Stop.' He shook his head, slamming the light off and stepping out in the hall so decisively that she almost stumbled in her effort to back up. 'I don't need to hear any more. You can come home with me.'

'What?' It felt as if all the air had been sucked

out of her lungs in a single instant. 'No. That's ridiculous.'

'No more ridiculous than what I've heard to-night,' Linc growled. 'You're camping on the couch and living off packet noodles, meanwhile I have a two-bed apartment, and a fridge full of fresh food.'

'I'm not staying with you.' She shook her head, horrified. 'I can't.'

Though whether at the idea of it, or at the way her body was reacting so entirely inappropriately, she couldn't be sure.

'Don't be a martyr, Piper,' he rasped. 'You can't stay here, and you clearly don't have much money if you're trying to support your mother and brother. The bedrooms at my place are opposite ends of the apartment, and we'll be here much of the time. You can stay just until the landlord has sorted your own place.'

She wanted to object, to politely decline. The idea of being in such close proximity to Linc seemed like a terrible one. Not to mention the wound it inflicted on her pride, having to rely on him like this.

But pride was no match for the crushing weight of responsibility. There was no doubt that even if she paid Linc something towards her stay, a week with him would be a lot cheaper than a week in a hotel. Especially around here.

Without doubt, her mother could use that money a handful of times over.

'Okay.' She nodded at last, stuffing back her unwanted sense of pride. 'Thank you. It would really help my family.'

And she pretended to herself that there wasn't a single part of her that was being tempted by entirely un-practical motives.

Not one single part of her, at all.

CHAPTER SIX

LINC HAD NO idea what he was doing. He'd invited her to his apartment...to *live* with him. Temporary or not, it had to be the most insane suggestion he'd ever made. The veneer of professionalism had well and truly slipped.

He could dress it up in the excuse that he was doing a good turn for a colleague in need, but the reality was that he found the idea of her actually being here...*thrilling.*

And wasn't that a concern all in itself?

He watched from the kitchen as she made her way around the living area, taking in his apartment's open-plan layout, double-height ceilings, and full-height windows on three sides, and he found he actually cared what she thought of it.

Not that he was going to tell her that he'd designed it himself—or that his family business had built several of the striking, sleek, glass and steel tower blocks in this area of the city. Yet still, he couldn't help wondering whether it was something that she liked.

He couldn't explain why her opinion mattered.

'When you said apartment, you didn't say it was a penthouse that covered the entire floor,' she muttered, after a long moment.

'Does it matter?'

She turned to look at him, wrinkling her nose, but she didn't answer.

'Some warning might have been nice.'

'Why? What would it have changed?' he asked easily. 'You needed a place to stay, and I have a spare room.'

She glowered at him but still didn't answer. It was crazy how much of a kick her little show of defiance caused in him. A return to the confident, fiery Piper he'd once known, instead of this smaller version of herself that he'd been beginning to see around the heli base.

'Why does it bother you so much, Legs?' he asked her, without warning. As if the nickname could ground them again.

She cast him a dark look.

'It doesn't.'

'That's clearly a lie.'

Piper chewed on the inside of her lip for a moment. Then shrugged.

'Do any of the crew know you live like some kind of millionaire?'

'Hardly,' he replied tightly. 'But no, the subject has never come up.'

'Just as it never did in the army?' she challenged. 'I think you deliberately hide this side of your life.'

'Like you hiding the fact that you've been supporting your family all this time?' He tried turning the tables, but all she did was lift one delicate shoulder.

'Something like that.'

A simple admission that reminded him there was more to Piper that he didn't know—and that roused his curiosity far more than it had any right to. They eyed each other, almost warily.

Still, now wasn't the time.

'Perhaps I should show you to your room?' he suggested instead.

She spun around a little too quickly, a telltale ragged pulse beating at her throat. He tried not to notice the way her pupils dilated, turning her amber eyes a much darker shade, or the slight flaring of her nostrils that betrayed her.

Responses that were all so deliciously...base— despite all their drawing lines in the sand. And Linc knew he shouldn't feel that punch of triumph—but it reverberated through him all the same.

But that didn't mean he was about to give in to such temptation.

Without waiting for her to catch up to him, he stepped from the open area to the hallway and strode along the plush corridor to the left. Dutifully, Piper followed him.

'Guest suite is down that way.'

'And...your master suite.'

'Back up on the other side of the living area,' he assured her. 'Just like I promised.'

'Right,' she managed, clearly a little shocked. 'This place is incredible.'

Something pulled in his chest at the unexpected note of self-censure in her voice. As though she felt she'd failed in some way.

'I've been here a while.'

'Whilst I can't even afford a hotel room right now.' She shook her head.

Guilt stabbed through him. Clearly their very different circumstances were some sort of deep-seated issue for Piper that he'd never quite appreciated before now.

'It's no failing, Piper. For a start, doctors get paid more than pilots in the military, we both know that,' he noted. 'At least at our respective levels.'

'I understand that...' She bit her lip again. And he hated that she somehow thought less of herself.

But he could hardly tell her who he really was. Linc cleared his throat, searching for an easy way to explain it away.

'I've also made money by dabbling in the stock markets. It's a bit of a hobby.'

Which was true enough. He was good at it too; it was a hobby the duke had taught him as a child on his knee.

'I wouldn't even know where to start with stock markets.' She shook her head. 'I never realised how very...different we are.'

And he knew as soon as she said it that she

hadn't meant for that to come out, even if he couldn't fathom why this all seemed to matter so much to her. Why, at least in her mind, she was drawing a division between them. Why she was highlighting the differences between them, and using that as an excuse to keep their distance from each other.

He found that it was his *not understanding* that rankled so much, and it occurred to him that distance was the last thing he wanted from this woman.

What the hell was wrong with him?

'Not so different.' Linc shrugged, deliberately playing it down. 'You learned to fly helis as a seventeen-year-old, around your family estate, did you not?' Although come to think of it, if that was the case, what had happened to that estate?

She eyed him oddly, and he had the distinct impression that there was a war going on in her head.

'No, I didn't, actually.'

'Oh?' He frowned. 'I thought I heard it mentioned back on that last tour of duty.'

'The two other female pilots on that tour had learned that way. And, given how every other pilot in the entire corps were men, they assumed I'd learned that way too. I stood out enough without telling them I wasn't a product of boarding school or super-rich parents, so it was easier just to let them think that I was like the other two females.'

'It was about fitting in?'

Even as he said it, a few other pieces of the puzzle he hadn't realised he'd started began to fall into place.

The way she'd always kept herself to herself; the way she'd never quite looked comfortable socialising with some of her peer group.

Had the military been an escape for Piper the way it had been for him—albeit for different reasons? She'd been running away from who she was, whilst he'd been running away from who he wasn't. As ironic as that was.

After his mother had pulled the proverbial rug from under him, he'd lost his identity. Joining the military as a doctor had given him back a sense of purpose, and a sense of worth. If it had somehow done the same for Piper, then no wonder they'd always felt that pull towards each other.

But wasn't that all the more reason to keep that proverbial line between them?

'Go and settle in,' he advised, not quite recognising the rasp in his own voice. 'Freshen up, get some sleep, whatever you need. Help yourself to anything in the kitchen. Tomorrow night I'll cook for us.'

And maybe they could finally find a way to be more comfortable around each other. Before the entire crew began to think there was more going on than there actually was.

* * *

Piper closed the door behind her and leaned
against it, her hand moving instinctively to her
ribcage as though she could slow down her racing
heart. It felt as though it was going at about Mach
10, and she knew it couldn't handle the G-forces.

She'd never been able to handle her attraction
to Linc; it was one of the reasons she'd been so
firm about drawing that professional line between
them, five years ago.

Yet it had been easier to do back then, on a
tour of duty, with all the military rules and pro-
tocols. Now, by contrast, the only rules, the only
boundaries, were self-imposed. And it was getting harder and harder to enforce them. She was
terribly afraid that here, in such close proximity
with no colleagues as buffers, that invisible line
was going to disappear altogether.

Worse, she wanted it to.

Pushing back off the door, Piper took a step into
the space. Belatedly, she realised that she wasn't
standing in a bedroom, she was standing in a private living room. A generous space with a couch,
and an antique study desk, and a breathtaking
view of the city below occupying one wall. Solid
doors occupied the other three walls, the double
set she'd entered through, and opposite was another double set. Carefully—as if she were afraid
she might intrude on a stranger in the space—she
padded around.

The two single doors opened up on a bathroom and a dressing room that were each probably the size of the main bedroom in the terraced house she'd bought for her mother. She doubted her entire wardrobe would have filled even one of the bespoke cabinets in the dressing room, whilst the travertine-tiled bathroom was like something out of a high-end, glossy hotel brochure.

She eyed the enormous bathtub—clearly designed for couples—and wondered whoever had the time for a bath. Growing up in her childhood home, and then in the military, showers had been de rigueur, and she'd never really missed the long soak that so many other women seemed to enjoy.

Now, however, the bath seemed to call to her. Piper moved falteringly forward, flipping the taps and watching a stream of hot, inviting water flow out. A peek into a small basket on the honed, polished counter top revealed a selection of spa products, and she selected one at random and dropped it almost nervously into the bath. The scent was instantly relaxing.

Feeling a little more confident, she made her way back through the room, piling her hair onto her head and snagging it into place. And then she allowed herself a little flourish as she pushed open the set of double doors that surely had to lead to the bedroom.

Her breath actually caught in her throat.

The room itself was the size of an entire floor

of her house. It had walls, a floor and a ceiling, but the similarities ended there. A huge bank of windows flooded the room with light, making it feel even more spacious and inviting. It took her a moment to realise that a set of patio doors led onto a wide balcony with gleaming oak wood decking, and a sleek metal and glass balustrade that offered tantalising views of the city beyond.

Piper stepped outside on autopilot, drawn to the spectacular sight. Like a carpet of land right at her feet. It made her feel free and powerful being up here and looking down on the city. As if she could do anything, conquer anything.

No wonder Linc loved it up here.

More than that, it allowed her to feel so far removed from her ordinary life that she could almost imagine she was a different person. Not herself. Without thinking, she followed the balustrade as it ran around the outside, lured by the sights as well as by the warm afternoon sun.

Then, tilting her face up towards it, the brightness making up for the lack of summer heat, Piper spread her hands out on the smooth wooden balcony rail and inhaled deeply.

Perfect relaxation.

'I assume you do know that you're outside my bedroom?'

The dry voice had her spinning around in an instant, fumbling for her words.

'What? Oh…no.'

Piper stopped dead. Linc was wearing nothing more than a pristine white towel around his waist, and his hair was slick, evidently from a shower. And everything become a hundred times worse. That hypersonic boom in her chest reverberating loudly—too loudly—in her head.

She couldn't seem to peel her eyes from the solid wall of his body, no matter how fiercely her brain screamed at her that she should. She'd always known he was muscled, the way his clothes had always clung so lovingly to him—from his army combats to his flight suit—had made that clear, but to see him in the flesh, naked, was a whole different ball game.

Like staring at the model for one of the great classical sculptures. A study in sheer masculinity.

Piper swallowed hard, desperately scrambling for something, anything, to say.

'You got a shower,' she managed to choke out at length.

Well, *accuse*, really. As though he didn't have the right to do what he liked in his own home.

'I did,' Linc agreed. 'I'd imagine you'd want to do the same, after a day like today.'

'I do.' She nodded, a little emphatically. 'That is, I usually do. But I saw that bath and I thought… I mean, it's clearly a bath for two.'

If the balcony had crashed under her feet and plummeted her down to ground level, she didn't think she'd have minded. In fact, she would probably have welcomed it. Wincing, she chanced a glance at Linc. Sure enough, he looked stony-faced.

'I mean… I didn't…' She felt more flustered than she thought she'd ever felt in her life. 'That wasn't supposed to sound like…'

'An invitation for me to join you?' he finished for her—grimly, she thought. 'No, I didn't imagine that it was.'

'Of course not,' she managed.

Liar, whispered that traitorous part of her body that was already starting to go molten at the mere suggestion.

'I don't normally indulge in baths, you understand.' Her mouth kept talking and she couldn't seem to stop it. 'I know it's probably not environmentally friendly…and sharing a bath is probably better in that sense…'

She tailed off awkwardly as Linc looked all the more pained.

'I think…perhaps…' She struggled to work her jaw. 'I think I should go to bed. It has been a long day, and the past few nights haven't been the most restful.'

'Then I hope you enjoy a relaxing bath,' he managed tightly. Gruffly.

'Yes. I…ought to get back to it.'

Evidently, this proximity to a practically naked Linc was frying her brain in a way that was more than a little embarrassing.

'I think that's for the best,' he rumbled as Piper grasped at the excuse to leave.

It was crazy how out of control she felt here, alone with him. With no military and no Helimed to act as a buffer, she felt fairly certain she was perilously close to losing her mind.

Either that, or she would lose every shred of her dignity, throwing herself at Linc the way she didn't seem to be able to stop herself.

Even as she scurried along the balcony, his low, rumbling voice seemed to chase her all the way back into her suite. And it didn't matter how firmly she slid the glass doors closed, it couldn't keep out that heavy ache in her chest. And lower, if she was going to be honest.

Swinging the bathroom door closed, then locking it, Piper hauled off her clothes and proceeded to drop them unceremoniously into the woven basket she always used as a laundry bag. The one that her mother had made for her before her first ever tour of duty. The one that, no matter where Piper was, always made her feel like home. Then, at last, she turned off the taps, stepped into the oversized tub and slid blissfully beneath the water, lying back and finally closing her eyes.

Slowly, slowly, the water lapped soothingly over her skin as the heat eased away the tensions of the day. Without warning, images of Linc exploring her body flew into her brain.

With a start, she lurched forward in the bath,

making the water slosh precariously up the sloped sides. She ought to be embarrassed, having such sinful thoughts about the man.

Instead, she couldn't seem to stop them.

Reaching for the loofah she'd already set out on the side, she began to scrub crossly at her skin.

Linc was spoiling everything. Being alone with him was definitely very different from working with him, and coming here had been a mistake, she told herself furiously.

So why didn't the rest of her body seem to believe that one bit?

CHAPTER SEVEN

PIPER WAS RUNNING through her pre-flight checklist the next morning and flushing the engine compressor section with de-ionised water, when Linc entered the hangar. And before she could stop it, her chest leapt in some kind of misplaced anticipation.

'I feel perhaps that I owe you an apology,' he declared without preamble. 'For last night.'

'Shh.' Automatically she glanced around the empty space before taking a step towards him.

A mistake, she realised instantly.

That stony look threatened his face again, and she tried not to take it as a kind of unspoken rejection.

'There's no one here, Piper. They're all in the crew room, or rec room, I checked.'

'Of course you did.' She scrunched up her nose.

'Listen, I offered you a place to stay because I wanted to help. I apologise if I made you feel awkward, or uncomfortable in any way.'

'You didn't,' she replied quickly.

She'd done that all by herself—by having such wholly inappropriate thoughts about him.

'Well, I hope that's true.' He inclined his head.

'I want you to feel you can relax. And stay as long as you need to.'

'Thank you,' Piper managed, fighting the urge to run her tongue all over her suddenly parched mouth.

No doubt Linc intended to be kind. Chivalrous. But, crazily, that only made him all the more appealing to her. Somehow it was easier to resist Linc when he was being a devilish playboy, rather than this solicitous, softer man.

Easier to resist? a voice mocked in her head. And that fraught knot in her stomach pulled tighter.

'I also wanted you to know that I'm going out tonight. So you'll have the place to yourself, just in case that makes things easier.'

It didn't. Not at all. Something sliced through Piper and she told herself it couldn't possibly be jealousy.

Definitely not.

'Thank you for letting me know,' she managed stiffly, instead. 'Should I...?'

She stopped abruptly, hating herself for caring where he was going. Or who with.

Linc frowned at her.

'Should you...?'

It would be better to shake it off and make some kind of joke. But Piper found she couldn't. She needed to know.

'Should I make myself scarce? In the morning? In case they think we're…'

He eyed her incredulously.

'I'm not going on a date, if that's what you think.'

'Oh.' She forced herself to sound casual. 'Well, okay, but, for the record, I don't expect you to curtail your private life. It isn't any of my business, and I don't care either way.'

He skewered her with the intensity of his gaze, and she forgot how to breathe.

And then, without warning, he took a step towards her.

'Do you really not care?' he murmured, moving his face closer to hers.

So close that she could feel his warm breath caressing her cheek, and it was all she could do to fight some ridiculous impulse to lean forwards and press her lips to his.

'Not at all.'

Maybe she would have sounded more convincing if her voice hadn't cracked, right at that moment. Fire burned in her cheeks, then spread over every inch of her skin. And still, she couldn't move.

'You lie like a cheap NAAFI watch,' he muttered suddenly.

'I'm not lying,' she croaked before snapping her mouth shut.

She feared she revealed more and more of herself with every unguarded thing she uttered.

'For what it's worth,' Linc drawled slowly, 'I'm meeting my sister. She's flying in tonight and we're having dinner to talk about what she expects of me for her wedding. So, no date. Not that that matters to you, I know.'

'I see,' she managed, and she hated herself for the way her heart soared at his words. 'But it still isn't my business.'

'True, but still, now you know,' he murmured before turning to head for the doors. 'I'll get back before anyone comes looking for me and finds me here.'

'Thank you,' she gritted out.

'Unless you want me to be your second for the two-person checks?'

There was another kick in her ribcage.

As the critical care doctor, Linc wasn't the designated data pilot, and therefore no one could reasonably expect him to run through the checks with her. Offering to be the stand-in now would certainly give them a legitimate excuse to be in here together for a little longer. But she really shouldn't read into the fact that he was offering to do so.

Was it a test? If she really didn't care where he went or who he dated, should she say she'd wait for the data pilot and tell him to leave?

'Well, you do happen to be here now,' she heard herself reply instead. 'And the sooner this thing is first paraded, the sooner she's ready for any shout.'

She could pretend it was about practicality all she liked, she suspected they both knew the truth. Still, picking up the digital notepad, Piper cast her eye over the stats for the heli.

'It won't hurt to just give a final check to the bowsers outside, either,' she told him. 'With the charity day coming up, and several longer-distance flights to get to events, we should ensure they have enough fuel of their own if we can't access the airport's main supply for any reason.'

'Good plan,' he agreed. 'Then we should probably also check the medical supplies, since we're both here.'

'Probably.'

And what did it say that the idea of being alone with Linc, with the safety net of work, seemed more than a little appealing?

For the next half-hour or so, they worked quickly and efficiently together, prepping the supplies and kit for the shift ahead. The easy banter between them seeping back in as the work tasks diluted the tension that had been building around them. It was a welcome breather.

They were about five minutes from the official shift start, and about to head over for a mug of tea, when the red phone sounded across the base. Hugo raced over a few moments later to pass on the details.

A twelve-year-old who had been thrown from her horse on a stretch of narrow country lane.

'We're good to go,' Piper acknowledged, grabbing her helmet and heading out onto the tarmac to get her heli started.

Within moments Tom had joined her, pulling up the map and punching in the grid reference, passing on the location details that had initially been transmitted.

'You're all clear for lift, Helimed hotel one-niner,' the ATC voice crackled over the headset.

'Thanks,' Piper acknowledged as she got her bird into the sky before banking sharply.

'I'd suggest following the main A road up to the supermarket roundabout, then follow the country land from there,' Linc's voice came over through her headset. 'This is the third accident in the same location this year—usually the drivers were morning commuters taking a short cut to bypass traffic on the motorway. They hurtle along the country road, don't observe the speed limit drop from sixty to twenty on this particular section where there are several sets of stables and a dairy farm, and end up screeching their tyres trying to stop when they round the bend to find a herd of cows crossing the road, or horses just coming off the end of the bridleway.'

'That's going to spook the animals,' Piper noted grimly, duly turning the nose to follow the A road. 'You know the best place to land, too?'

'Yeah, there's a field just to the left as we head to location. Albert usually lands there, and there's a decent gap in the wall, so it's easy enough to get out, as well as bring the patient back through.'

'Sold,' she confirmed, concentrating on getting them there quickly as the radio crackled again.

'This is hotel zero seven, we have an update on the casualty,' Hugo's voice told them. 'Twelve-year-old female was thrown from her horse. Landed on the undergrowth and was unconscious for about a minute. She has been confused ever since. No other injuries reported.'

'Update received, out,' Linc acknowledged, addressing his team as Hugo ended the update. 'We'll check her over head-to-toe anyway, of course, but it seems we're looking at assessing whether she's suffering from simple concussion or extradural haematoma.'

'I'll get the heli as close as possible,' Piper assured him. 'In case you need to get the casualty to a major trauma unit as quickly as possible. We're coming up on the location now.'

Bringing the heli around, she looked for the field Linc had mentioned.

Damn.

'It's a no-go for the landing,' she told him. 'There are livestock in the field.'

'Hell. They're usually in the area on the other side of the road.'

Piper cast her eye over in that direction.

'Well, one of those fields is clear, but the overhead wires on that side of the road are going to push us to the back corner.'

'Anyone see an exit point?' Linc asked quickly.

'Nothing on the left,' Tom advised after a moment. 'What about you, Probie?'

'I think there's a gate at the bottom corner of the field,' Probie advised carefully. 'Yes… I'm sure there is.'

'Good eye, Probie,' Linc's voice agreed after a moment. 'There's a gate leading to a dirt track which joins the country lane itself. Wait a moment…yeah, there's someone running over that way now, waving. Land here, Piper. You're clear on the tail.'

'Left is good,' Tom agreed, as Probie chimed in that the right side was also clear.

Slowly bringing the heli down, Piper nosed down the field before finally letting the skids touch the ground.

'You're as close as I can get,' she told them, as the team all started to move. 'But if you need me to move, just let me know.'

Then they were gone, and all she could do was sit. And wait.

Linc's mind was still on that last shout as he pulled on his shirt later that evening.

By the nature of what the air ambulance did, they were usually only called to serious cases, and his time with the army had exposed him to any number of horrific injuries. But cases involving kids were always worse.

Seeing such young patients—whose whole lives should be ahead of them—suffering life-changing injuries could be almost unbearable sometimes. Especially when, like that last shout, there had actually been nothing more for his team to do than to load the girl onto the heli and get her to hospital for the right scans.

The kid might not have had any external injuries that he and his team could patch up and help to heal, but it had been clear from her constant confusion that she'd suffered some kind of brain injury despite her riding helmet. And his team could do nothing about a head injury except get her to a major trauma unit as quickly as they could.

He hated that sense of helplessness. That feeling of not being able to *do* something to change the situation.

And now he was supposed to go out and enjoy an evening with his sister, albeit also endure her inevitable reprimands, as though everything were fine. Yet tonight was one of those nights when all he really wanted to do was stay here and maybe hit his home gym. Anything to expend the fraught feeling—the sense of frustration—that was slamming around inside him like a ball on a squash court.

But he had to go. He'd already delayed it to try to get his head back to reality, but he had to go. It was part of his responsibility to his family, to his sister. Hauling open his door, he stalked down the hall, picking up his mobile from the hall stand where he'd dropped it, and had his hand on the penthouse door when Piper emerged from her end of the hallway.

Linc dropped his hand without even meaning to.

Clad only in a short dressing gown that revealed acres of mouthwatering skin and offered yet more proof of why the nickname *Legs* was perfect for her, she sauntered up the corridor, her nose so buried in a book that she hadn't even noticed him.

His body reacted instantly. Viscerally.

As though it were traitorously exempt from whatever practical, cerebral agreement he and Piper had come to concerning not crossing any professional boundaries. Surely no red-blooded male could have failed to respond to the glorious sight of Piper? Though perhaps he would have fought his body's instinct a little harder had a part of him not welcomed the fact that it distracted from the sense of frustration he'd been feeling after the shout.

Piper was closer now, and still she hadn't noticed him. Dimly, he thought he ought to say something, or make a noise to alert her to his presence. But when he did, he barely recognised his own voice.

'Piper?'

She stopped short, the shock evident in her expression.

Her hair still wet and slick from the shower, her bare feet with the delicately painted pink toenails that he would never have believed if he weren't seeing them now.

The last thing Piper had ever seemed to him was soft, or pink—he found he rather liked seeing this unexpected softer side of her.

'I thought you were out,' she accused tightly, visibly swallowing.

He moved and her eyes dropped instantly to the small open V at the top of his shirt, and her tongue flicked out wickedly over her plump lips.

Rather as if she couldn't stop herself.

He felt a kick somewhere in his gut, revelling in the way she seemed to have to fight herself to lift her gaze back to his face.

'You're supposed to be at dinner by now,' she continued, in a strangled voice.

And he revelled in that, too.

'Not for about an hour. After the last shout, I called Sara and pushed the time back.'

Her expression grew pained, but her darkening pupils betrayed her. He knew women well enough to know that look. Moreover, he knew Piper well enough to know that look.

'You didn't tell me,' she accused. But hoarsely.

He couldn't help teasing her.

'And miss the show?' he rasped, his eyes sweeping slowly over her before he could stop himself.

He was rewarded instantly when her nipples tightened visibly beneath the soft fabric of the dressing gown, like a scorching lick of heat over the hardest part of himself. Even as his brain bellowed at him to back away—to maintain that divide between them—a far more base, more carnal sound roared through his body. And the longer he sinfully indulged in her, the more that fraught knot in his gut began to slip undone.

The devil on his shoulder whispered how easy it would be to call his sister and cancel their meeting altogether just to stay here with Piper so they could make their own entertainment.

His head filled all too easily with images of her wrapped around his body. Not to mention those tantalising glimpses of soft skin that kept peeking out from beneath the collar of her silky dressing gown.

As if reading his mind, she clutched it a little closer to preserve her modesty. But those darkening eyes, that ragged breathing, told a different story.

'I was planning on getting something to eat and going to bed early.' She managed to sound prim yet sexy all at the same time.

A true skill, Linc rather thought. He took a step towards her, and watched that pulse flutter manically at the base of her neck.

Crying out to him.

'That sounds like a wise idea,' he ground out. 'I would do the same if I could.'

'You're going out.' Piper's voice was hoarse.

'I am,' he acknowledged, battling the urge to take another step towards her.

He succeeded. But that didn't mean he was ready to take a step towards the door.

'It was a difficult day,' she murmured, after a moment.

'It was.'

'Do you think the kid will be okay?'

'I hope so,' he muttered. 'I hope she regains her memory quickly.'

'Sometimes, it's easy to forget how short life can be.'

'And get caught up in the rules?' His gaze held hers. 'The idea of what's right, or what's appropriate?'

'I guess…that's what I'm saying.' She hesitated, and he tried to quash the sense of victory that rolled towards him.

'Do you want me to stay?' he demanded, the rasp in his tone seeming to echo around the room.

Her eyes darkened and she moved one single step in his direction before seeming to stop herself.

'I…your sister is waiting.'

And he tried to cling onto the logical, practical argument that said they should keep their distance, but there was no quashing his triumph this time. It punched through him. Loud, and vibrant.

'How tempted are you?' he heard himself demand.

'Who says I'm tempted?' she replied on a choppy whisper—wholly undermined by the way her body leaned towards him.

'That isn't precisely an answer,' he managed, his voice raw, his body jolting at the way her breath caught audibly. 'Are you as tempted as I am? More?'

Linc couldn't have said who moved first, but abruptly the gap between them closed, and her body was against his, and fighting temptation was no longer a question. Something else was in control of them now: the attraction, the lust, that they'd been staving off for weeks—for years, if they included back in the army.

Finally, *finally*, he slid his fingers through her damp hair and set his mouth to hers, glorying in the way she lifted her hands and seemed to simply…cling on, and the fire licked at him in an instant.

It moved through him, getting higher and hotter as she let him angle her head for a better fit, testing first this way and then that way, seeming to melt against him that little bit more with every delicious slide of his tongue against hers.

Dully, he was aware of a mobile phone ringing in the background, but he didn't care. Scooping her up, his hands cupping that perfectly toned backside, he carried her over to the kitchen countertop and sat her down. Was it him, or her, who wrapped her legs around his waist to pull him in, just a few layers of fabric separating her soft, wet heat from the very hardest part of his body, just like in every dirty dream he'd ever had about her?

And he liked that carnal sound she made, low in her throat, when he told her as much.

And still, he wasn't even sure she meant to move and yet her hands lifted up between them until her palms were spread gloriously over his chest. So that the pulse in her thumb was right over the drumming of his heart.

He shifted and she moaned against his mouth, pressing her breasts to him, so tightly that he could feel how proud and pert her nipples were. His mouth watered. The need to take her, to claim her, was almost painful. This thing they'd shared had been arcing between them for so long. But he was determined not to rush. To take it slow.

Slowly, with painstaking deliberation, he slid his hand down to cup the base of her head, tipping it back so that he could feast on the long, elegant line of her neck, relishing the way she shivered in response and leaned back further to grant him better access.

He couldn't have said what it was about the scrabbling outside—perhaps the unusualness of the sound, perhaps his subconscious had been expecting something the moment his phone had started its incessant ringing—that alerted him something was wrong moments before the door to his apartment swung open.

And all he could do was shove Piper behind him, his first thought preserving whatever he could of her modesty.

CHAPTER EIGHT

PIPER HAD BARELY registered what was going on as Linc pulled her down from the countertop and set her firmly behind him just as a woman—a stunning woman, to be precise—strode into the room.

Linc's sister, presumably.

The woman stopped abruptly when she saw them. But rather than looking embarrassed or shocked, she looked angry. With an odd undercurrent of…curiosity.

By contrast, Piper found all the self-confidence she'd had to finally kiss Linc seeped out of her in an instant. She wasn't even certain she could remember how to breathe.

'What the hell do you think you're doing, Sara?' Linc growled, clearly not suffering from the same lack of confidence.

Any other woman—any other person—would have cowed at the unmistakeably dangerous edge to his tone. Even Piper found herself desperate to move, but unable to budge. Embarrassment and anger were waging their own little war inside her head, and she wasn't yet certain which was going to win.

Sara, however, barely even flinched.

'You weren't answering your phone,' she continued, her focus on Linc. 'I didn't think you were home.'

'So you just let yourself in?'

He advanced on her, clearly furious, but the woman just jerked her chin up at him as only a sister could.

'You gave me a key.' She lifted her immaculately tailored shoulders in a gesture too elegant to be considered as unsophisticated as a shrug.

'For emergencies,' Linc growled, but his sister seemed to ignore that, too.

'We were supposed to be meeting for dinner earlier.'

'I called you to tell you I was running late from our last shout.'

'By which time I was already in the air,' his sister noted disdainfully. 'Coming here seemed like the logical solution. Was I supposed to divine the fact that the reason you pushed our meal back an hour was because you're...otherwise engaged.'

Sara scrunched up her nose, evidently unimpressed, and despite her best efforts Piper couldn't stop the heat from flooding her cheeks at the loaded accusation. But in the war between shame and anger, the latter was beginning to win out.

'We didn't...that is... I'm not the reason...' Piper began in a clipped voice before Linc took over for her.

'Piper had nothing to do with me pushing the meeting time back tonight.'

And Piper wondered if she was the only one to notice that slightly thicker note to his tone. Whether she was the only one who understood the reason behind it, that sense of helplessness as they'd flown that confused twelve-year-old kid—who couldn't even remember her name, or that it was her birthday that very day—to the hospital.

'I think I ought to leave,' Piper managed.

'Good idea,' Linc's sister agreed coldly.

But as Piper began to move out from around Linc—her state of undress be damned—Linc snaked his hand around to protect her.

'I'll walk with you,' he murmured reassuringly, before turning his attention back to his sister. 'This is my home, Sara, you don't speak to my guests like that. And you certainly don't send her scuttling back to her bedroom like some chastened child.'

'Her bedroom?' his sister echoed in disbelief. 'She's living here?'

'Staying temporarily.' There was no hint of apology in Linc's voice. 'Not that it's your business, but for Piper's sake I'm telling you that she's our emergency pilot since our usual one was in an accident. Since she's from out of the area, she found herself without accommodation.'

'Of course she did.' The sarcasm was unmistakeable. 'And I can see the attraction, I can, Lincoln. But moving her in with you? You aren't pregnant, are you?'

This last bit was patently directed at her, but Piper didn't get chance to respond before Linc had dropped his arm from around her waist, and advanced on his sister.

This time, he didn't think there was any way he was reining in his anger.

'Too far, Sara,' he growled, as he took his sister firmly, though not harshly, by the shoulders, and began to propel her swiftly to the exit. And Piper thought the woman must have realised she'd overstepped because, this time, she didn't argue.

But, at the last moment, another man appeared in the doorway.

'Is there a problem?'

His low voice rumbled through the penthouse, sounding so achingly familiar that Piper had to twist her head around to check that it hadn't come from Linc himself.

In an instant, every line of Linc's body changed. He stopped ejecting his sister as she thrust out her hand to the door jamb and spun herself around, whilst Linc folded his arms over his body.

'I didn't know you were coming,' he told the other man, and Piper thought it was interesting how his attitude had changed.

Clearly this was someone who mattered to Linc, who he cared about—his older brother, Raf, perhaps? The man certainly had an air of quiet authority about him that was so similar to Linc. Plus, even though she'd never met him, the way Linc had always talked about him, it had been clear that he respected and loved his brother. She'd always known when he'd managed a video call with his brother from out there, in that theatre of war. Linc had always seemed to be much more settled and grounded for weeks afterwards.

Though she'd never really bothered to ask herself why Linc's state of mind had always been so important to her.

'I told you what I need to discuss with you is important,' Sara announced now, triumphant as her glance encompassed the other man. 'Why else would Raf have come?'

So it *was* Linc's brother, Raf.

At least her own presence here had been apparently forgotten, for the moment. Piper wondered if she could slip away unnoticed.

'About the optics of your wedding,' Linc was saying to his sister as Piper inched towards the hallway to her suite—not that she dared break cover from behind the countertop. 'Isn't it always, these days?'

Despite the circumstances, Piper winced on Sara's behalf at the evident disdain in Linc's voice. Linc didn't mean to, that much was clear, but his dismissal of his sister's wedding clearly hurt her, though she rallied impressively. And even though Piper knew it probably wasn't her place to comment, nonetheless, she made a mental note to mention it to him when they were alone again.

'It's about more than just me, Linc,' Sara pleaded.

'I know what it's about,' he scoffed. 'It's always the same.'

And this time, when Sara bit back, Piper could almost understand it.

'No, you don't, because you never listen, and you never bother to come home. Tonight is a prime example. Apparently, Raf—' she spun again, this time to look at her other brother '—the reason Linc decided to make us wait this evening is because he was otherwise occupied with his new... houseguest. *Piper*.'

And as easy as that, the woman was back to a barely concealed contempt that cut right through Piper.

'That's enough, Sara,' Linc bit out, with audible fury in his tone. 'That's your last warning.'

And though she appreciated him defending her, Piper could only wish the ground would open up and swallow her whole. Anything to get away from the scrutiny—and the disdain.

For all the confidence she had in her career, and on the battlefield, she'd never found it easy to deal with strangers. Especially those who were clearly monied, and accustomed to throwing their wealth around. Like this woman.

Now, as much as it galled Piper to admit it, Linc's siblings were making her feel smaller and smaller with each passing moment. She certainly wasn't prepared for the brother's reaction.

'Wait… Piper?' he mused, as though the name meant something to him.

A dull drumbeat started up in Piper's chest, though she told herself that she shouldn't read too much into it. She mustn't.

'You served with Lincoln, didn't you?' the brother pondered. 'A few years ago?'

'Just around five years,' Piper forced herself to answer.

'Is that right?' Sara interjected. 'And now you're here and living with my brother, though we've never been formally introduced.'

Her tone was pointed, but Linc wasn't having any of it.

'Nor will you be now,' he gritted out, moving back to be closer to Piper. Half shielding her, half lending her strength.

'It would be good to remedy it, though,' his brother stated evenly. 'Perhaps Piper would like to get changed and accompany us to dinner.'

'I don't think so.' Linc didn't even hesitate, meanwhile Sara was gasping with obvious dismay.

'Raf…this is family business.'

'Sara, you've been rude enough already,' her older brother chastised. 'Linc and Piper have both been more than patient and I think we can all agree that these aren't the circumstances under which any of us would have chosen to meet. I think going for a meal together would help to remedy that. Would you not agree?'

And even though Raf was looking at both of them, Piper could tell that his focus was on his brother.

This was a test. Raf was using the invitation to gauge his brother's feelings towards her.

And even though a part of her wanted to jump in and tell both siblings that she and Linc were just friends, she found herself waiting for Linc to speak. Steeling herself—though she didn't care to examine why—for the moment he told them that she had no place joining them.

Slowly, she dragged her eyes from Raf, and Sara, to rest on Linc. Preparing herself for the inevitable. And, at last, he responded.

'The choice is yours, Piper,' he told her slowly. Thoughtfully. 'Would you care to join us?'

Shock walloped into her. She didn't need to look at Linc's brother to know what he was reading into the moment—not that she could have dragged her gaze from Linc even if she'd tried—and she could certainly hear the sharp intake of breath from his sister.

What was Linc even playing at? He might as well have announced some intention to commit himself to her. It was certainly what it sounded like. She couldn't explain it. Certainly couldn't understand it.

She opened her mouth to tell him that she would

be spending the night here, with her bath and early night as planned.

'Give me a few minutes to change,' she heard herself say instead.

And then, with a confidence that she hadn't known she'd had before—at least outside a helicopter cockpit, she stepped out from behind the counter, and strode as casually as she could across the hallway and down to her guest suite.

Let them make of that whatever they would.

It only took her a few moments to push herself off the closed door, where she'd been leaning and trying to catch her breath. She didn't have long to get ready if she didn't want to irk Linc's siblings— notably his sister—any more than she already had.

There was no pretending that she hadn't noticed the critical way that Sara had eyed her up and down, leaving her feeling as if she were a dog, or a horse, rather than a human. Only Sara probably would have shown more interest and care if she *were* of the four-legged variety.

She still didn't know what had possessed Linc to invite her; less still why she'd accepted, but at least she was grateful that she'd already showered. There might not be enough to time to blow-dry her hair the way she might have preferred, but she was accustomed to deftly twisting it up into an elegant chignon, and brushing on a quick hint of make-up.

As for her clothes, she didn't have much choice.

Her go-to evening wear was a pair of flowing black trousers—her only non-work pair, in fact, but she liked that they seemed to make her more glamorous, less gangly—and a pretty top that she'd brought on the off-chance of going out for an evening.

And she told herself that Linc definitely hadn't been in her mind when she'd been standing in front of her locker in barracks, taking that particular top off its hanger.

It would have to do. Nothing that she had would come anywhere close to the exquisite creation that Linc's sister had appeared to be wearing, but at least she would feel sufficiently dressed-up to hold her own at whatever restaurant they seemed to be booked into.

Linc was still trying to work out why the heck he hadn't shut his brother down when he'd invited Piper to join them for the evening.

He'd known it had been a test. Clearly, he'd failed it. By allowing the situation to play out he'd left his siblings with the impression that there was something going on between him and Piper.

Isn't there? a voice taunted in his head, before he could shut it down.

The fact remained that he'd needlessly opened Piper up to more scrutiny, and he only had himself to blame.

'I still don't understand what she's even doing

here.' Sara flounced across the room and threw herself into one of the pristine dove-grey leather chairs in the living area.

'I told you, it's about practicality,' he repeated, though he was beginning to doubt that, even of himself. 'We're old friends, so when she needed somewhere to stay for a week or two, I was happy to oblige.'

'Yes, I can see how happy you are.'

If it hadn't been for Raf's presence, he wasn't sure he would have continued to indulge his sister. For all her prickliness he loved her intently but, had his brother not shown up, he would have happily ejected her from his penthouse the first time she'd been rude to Piper.

Even now, her snort of derision wound him up even tighter than before.

'You looked like a pair of guilty, libido-ridden teenagers standing there when I walked in. And, frankly, you were never that guilty as a teenager, Lincoln.'

'You're sailing close to the wind, Sara,' Linc growled.

A wiser person would have heeded the warning. His sister, however, actually waved her hand in the air even more derisively.

'You might not be a monk, dear brother, but I can count the number of dates you've had with the same woman on one hand. Now you're telling me that you've actually moved this *Piper* into your apartment?'

'I told you out of courtesy,' Linc replied coldly, 'but ultimately it isn't really any of your concern. Yours or Raf's.'

'It's entirely of our concern. Which you'd know if you'd take your head out of your backside long enough to listen to us. To come back and be the part of the family you've always been—'

'That will do, Sara,' Linc ground out, just as Raf uttered something along similar lines.

Sara spun around instantly.

'The point of this evening is to talk family matters with Linc. *Private* family matters. How can we do that with his "houseguest" in there?'

'Sara.' This time it was Raf who cut her off first. 'I know you're worried about the family company, but I've never known you to be so catty before. I can't say I care for it.'

Raf's tone was the perfect balance between commanding and caring. It was a skill that his brother had always known just how to execute, and one that Linc had long envied.

'I'm also worried about you,' she added stubbornly, before swinging back around to Linc, her eyes flashing. 'You do realise that two of the board members have been trying to topple Raf by secretly buying up shares and now have forty per cent. They're weeks away from organising a coup.'

'What does it matter?' Linc growled, his eye on the door to Piper's suite, beginning to regret his earlier decision. This was definitely not a conversation he wanted her to overhear. It would mean having to explain too much. 'So long as you, Raf and I stick together, they can never outvote us; we still hold the controlling interest.'

'Except that the devious bastards have managed to dig up some of the truth about you. About Mum. They've got a whiff of the fact that…well, you know…and he's going to use that against Raf.'

It was as if the world froze—his siblings, his penthouse, time itself.

'This isn't the place, Sara.' Linc was aware of Raf's censure, but it was too late.

It was said. The box was open. The thing the three of them never, *never* discussed swirled around the room.

'They know that the old duke isn't my father.' Linc wasn't sure how he managed to sound so calm. So in control. He felt anything but. 'Say the words, Sara.'

'They know,' she choked out. 'And they're using that to claim that your shares were never yours to inherit. They're trying to have you thrown off the board. The board votes next week.'

His tongue felt too big for his mouth. Too unwieldy. Yet somehow, he didn't know how, he spoke.

'Then let them. If that's the weapon he's using

to unseat Raf, let him use it. If the board votes me out, and claims I'm not a proper Oakes, then let them. They aren't wrong. The duke wasn't my biological father. I'm just your half-brother.'

It was as if every fear he'd ever had—the very reason for him leaving Stoneywell and not returning—was suddenly coming to pass. His past was rushing up on him, threatening to swallow him whole, and there was nothing he could do to hold it back.

'You *are* our brother.' Sara pushed herself up from her seat and flung herself at him furiously for a moment. 'I don't care what anyone else says or thinks.'

And it was ridiculous how touched he was at her unfailing love. The way she'd always been, even that first night their mother had so gleefully announced the truth about her infidelity. As loving and supportive as Raf, as their father, had been—even when she'd produced a DNA test to prove it, driven by some vicious compulsion to hurt the old duke that little bit more.

But somehow, that had only made it all the harder to accept. Because the more they had closed around him, the three of them in a protective ring around him—the more he'd felt as if he wasn't one of them. Like a cuckoo in their nest.

Ultimately, it had been their love that had pushed him to join the army to get away from them. Irony at its worst.

'He was our father. To all three of us,' Raf rasped out as Sara moved back to her own seat. 'I will not hear otherwise.'

'But if the argument is accepted, it will make things easier for you. My shares would just revert to you two. Those old cronies win nothing by getting rid of me, so let them do it.'

'That isn't the point,' Sara cried.

'I think it is,' argued Linc, as though his heart weren't cracking, right there in his soul.

'No,' Raf disagreed quietly. 'Besides, even if it were the point, there's more to it.'

'Meaning?'

'Meaning that they also know Daddy knew about the infidelity,' Sara revealed. 'And that you couldn't be his…biological son. So they're contesting his state of mind at the time his will was drawn up.'

'Say again?' Linc thundered, his head swirling with the revelations.

'They're saying that the Alzheimer's started earlier, and that decisions he made during the later years—the direction that the company took—might not have been taken had he been in his right mind.'

'He was in his right mind.' Linc frowned. 'He knew exactly what he was doing with the company, right up until those last few years. It's the same direction Raf has been taking the company—'

He stopped abruptly, his mind beginning to work through the noise.

'Which is precisely why they're using it as a means to get Raf out, too,' Sara bit out.

Linc turned to his brother.

'You can't let them get away with it.'

'I'm dealing with it,' Raf rumbled softly. Steadfastly.

Looking from one brother to the other, Sara threw her hands up in frustration.

'But it would be a whole lot easier if you came home and helped. Raf, will you please tell him that he needs to come home?'

Linc didn't know why he looked at his brother. Raf couldn't possibly need his help. His older brother was always so in control, so strong. And still, he watched, certainty turning to shock when Raf didn't instantly refute Sara's claim.

'It would...help,' his brother acknowledged after a moment.

There was little need to say anything more. For Raf to even say that much meant that they were in trouble. It was almost unconscionable.

'Most of the board members don't want a coup,' Sara pressed after a moment. 'They want the problem to just go away. And maybe it would, if you were home. If you were part of the business, just like you were always meant to be. Like we were all always meant to be.'

'I don't see what my presence would change,'

Linc growled, feeling even more of an imposter than ever.

'It would show your commitment to Stoney-well. To the family name, and the family business, just as Daddy always believed we would be.' His sister's voice trembled, somewhere between grief and ferocity.

Still, Linc shook his head.

'That won't change the facts. I'm still...who I am.'

Not his father's biological son.

'It would change things if you came back home and settled down. Maybe took on the role as Chief of the Stoneywell Medical Centre,' Sara pointed out. 'There are plenty of old-guard board members who supported Daddy, and who would like nothing better than for him to be proved right by the three of us running Oakenfeld Industries together, the way he had always envisaged.'

'I'm not a private practice doctor.' Linc hated that she was suggesting such a move. And hating himself even more for refusing to help. 'I'm a former army doctor. I'm an air ambulance doctor. I go where I'm needed, not where cash-splashing celebrities want me to be.'

'Then reconsider,' Sara snapped. 'For Raf, if not for yourself.'

'Raf doesn't need me. He can resolve this issue without my help,' Linc argued, even as several pieces began to topple into place. 'Is that what all your phone calls have been about? All this pressure to bring a plus one to your wedding rehearsal next week? To your wedding? You want me to pretend to the board that I'm finally settling down and thinking of coming back to the fold, a changed man?'

'It couldn't hurt,' his sister blasted.

He begged to differ. He'd never known a problem his older brother couldn't fix.

'It's fine, Linc.' His brother dipped his head, as though reading his mind. As in control as ever. 'I'll think of something. I still have a few plays in motion before next week.'

'Right,' Linc agreed.

But guilt still moved through him. If it was that easy, then Raf wouldn't be here in the first instance.

The glittering, shimmering tears in his sister's eyes didn't help, either.

'Since when did you get so selfish, Lincoln Oakes?' she choked out. 'All these years we've supported your choices, from the army to the air ambulance. But now we need you and…'

The click of the door down the hallway silenced whatever else his sister had been going to say, and he and his brother stood automatically as the surprising sound of high heels clicked down the marble flooring towards them.

And then it was his turn for the words to pile up

in his chest. Caught in the vacuum, every breath in him was sucked out.

Piper looked stunning. No, more than that, she looked positively majestic, standing in front of them like some kind of goddess, with the most dazzling smile falling from her lovely face.

And he thought only he could read the tiniest of tension marks around the normally smooth edges.

Mine, the shockingly primitive thought bellowed in his head. In his soul. *All mine.*

Then his remarkable Piper stepped towards his sister, her arm outstretched.

'Shall we try this again?' she asked lightly, almost breezily. 'I'm Piper. It's lovely to meet you, Sara. I've heard so much about you over the years, it's great to finally put a face to—'

'Lady Sara,' his sister cut across her with a smile of her own that was bright but sharp.

Instinct made him step forward.

'For God's sake, Sara,' he growled, moving to stand next to Piper, but it was too late. His gut pulled taut as Piper twisted to him, blinking in shock.

'Lady Sara?' she asked tightly.

'Just as my brother here is Lord Lincoln.' Sara's voice sounded muffled as he held Piper's gaze. 'Surely you understand that's how titles work?'

Tearing himself from Piper, he moved to his penthouse door and yanked it back open.

'Leave now, Sara,' Linc gritted out.

How had he not realised that his secret would be revealed if Piper spent any time with his siblings? Had he been so caught up with what had happened between them in the moments before his sister had walked in?

Regrettably, he realised the answer was *yes*.

'Titles?' Piper was still echoing, evidently stunned.

'Of course.' Sara was eying her curiously now. 'You'll understand my surprise that you're apparently living with my brother but claim not to even know that.'

'She didn't know.' Linc stepped in. 'And it really is time you left.'

'What about dinner?' Sara demanded.

'Goodbye, Sara,' Linc managed icily, his eyes on a reeling Piper. 'Go home. Go to dinner. But you will leave my home.'

'I have a better idea.' Raf stepped in calmly. 'Linc, you and Piper go to the restaurant, and talk on neutral ground. Clearly we've overstepped the mark here. I apologise. Sara, you and I are leaving.'

'No, but—'

'Now, Sara.' Raf ushered her to the door in much the way that Linc himself had before.

Linc was grateful. For all his own usual self-control, looking at Piper's ashen face at this moment, he could happily have kicked his sister out on her designer-clad backside.

'I'm glad to have met you.' Raf shook Piper's hand smoothly, even as he kept propelling Sara towards the door. 'I regret that it wasn't under better circumstances. Perhaps next time.'

And with those words hanging in the air like some kind of simultaneously unspoken criticism and assurance, Raf removed the two of them from the penthouse leaving Linc to finally be alone with the only woman he realised he could ever have imagined knowing his most guarded secret.

CHAPTER NINE

PIPER WAS STILL processing the revelations of the previous evening as she first paraded the helicopter the following morning. Hardly surprising, since she'd also been thinking about it all night; barely able to sleep.

They'd eaten at the finest restaurant Piper thought she'd ever been to. A ten-course tasting menu fit for the lords and lady that Linc and his siblings were.

But between the glazed scallop with salt-baked parsnips, nasturtium, and crisp pork belly starter, and the rich, mirror-glazed cocoa delight with edible gold leaf flecks for dessert, they'd also talked.

Linc, the man she'd known for years—the army doctor she'd served alongside on multiple tours—was a lord? It still seemed too crazy to be true.

He'd talked to her about his family's Oakenfeld Industries, and shared inheritances, he'd explained to her about Raf being the new Duke of Stoneywell, and given her a brief outline of the board members who were trying to topple his brother, but she still wasn't entirely sure that she understood all the facts, even now.

She hated his guilt that his abandonment of the family business had led to such instability, and a part of her could now begin to understand what his sister meant by using the optics of her wedding to make it appear that Linc was finally ready to settle down and return to the family fold.

But Piper couldn't shake the feeling that he was leaving out something more to the story. She couldn't escape the idea that there was a vital piece that he wasn't sharing.

Perhaps it was to do with the way his siblings had seemed much more open and receptive towards Linc than he had to them. As though there were a sheet of one-way glass between them, and Linc were on the protected side of it.

Five years ago, he'd given her the impression he would have moved heaven and earth for his brother and his sister. Now, she wasn't so sure. Part of her felt as though he wanted to…it was simply as though there was a wall stopping him. A wall that only Linc himself had built. She wished she understood it.

It all made her wonder if she'd ever really known him at all.

She'd been about to sleep with him—well, perhaps not *sleep,* precisely—and she hadn't even known the truth. Worse, she wasn't even sure a part of her cared. She, who had always told herself that she would never give herself to a man she couldn't be completely honest with.

Yet here she was, still wondering whether she was imagining something between herself and

Linc, or whether it really existed. Even lying in that luxurious guest bed last night, still reeling from the revelations, it had been like some form of exquisite torture—knowing that Linc had been only metres away, at the other end of the penthouse.

How could it be that he was sending her out of her mind on so many different levels?

It felt as though the more time she spent at his home, the more she wasn't sure she understood herself at all.

How was it he could leave her feeling so gloriously desirable, yet at the same time so damned easy to resist? No wonder the more time she spent in his penthouse, the more sexually frustrated she seemed to be feeling. She, who had never really considered herself to have a particularly high libido in general.

Which was surely why spending time with Linc intimately, even for pretend, was the last thing she should do?

'Hey, Piper, grub's up. My famous chilli.' Linc interrupted her thoughts, appearing at the door of the base just as she was finishing pulling the trailer back to the hangar. 'You okay?'

'Sure.' She regrouped quickly. 'I didn't know you were cooking.'

Because if he could pretend that everything was normal between them, then so could she.

No matter that it cost her dearly to do so.

But then he stayed by the door, as if there was something else on his mind.

'Something else you wanted to say?' she managed, impressing herself with how nonchalant she actually sounded.

Surely he couldn't hear that slight quiver in her voice?

'Have you heard the news about Albert?' he asked abruptly.

And there was no reason for her heart to plummet, but it did.

'What news?'

'Albert and Jenny are being discharged tomorrow. Jenny suffered a couple of fractured ribs from the steering wheel but nothing critical so she'll be laid up for a little while, but Albert got off with only a few minor injuries so he should be back within a fortnight.'

'That's great.' Guilt sliced through Piper at how hard it was to keep her smile bright.

'You could be back at barracks, away from here before you know it.'

'Even better,' she acknowledged, her smile so wide she feared her face might actually fracture.

She was pleased for the crew, obviously. The idea of any of them being injured wasn't one she would wish on anyone. At the same time, a part of her would have welcomed a little more time with Heathston Helimed.

With Helimed, or with Linc? that insidious little voice challenged. And even as she told herself the idea of leaving was only hard because the steady income was just what she needed to help her family—not any other reason, of course—she knew she didn't believe it.

For a moment, they seemed caught in time. Watching each other without a word. And then Linc spoke. Quietly, catching them both off guard.

'Is it, though?' he asked, making a move to close the gap between them.

She held her hands out palms up. Neither trying to stop him, nor caution him.

'Isn't it?'

Before he could answer, the alarm sounded for another shout. Wordlessly, they each sprang into action, as if the moment had never happened. But even as she leapt into the cockpit, she couldn't quite evict the thick feeling that squatted heavily on her chest.

By the sounds of it, she had a handful of shifts left here and then she would be gone. From Heathston Helimed...and from Linc's life.

'What's the call?' Piper demanded as the crew raced over the tarmac and to her heli.

'Road traffic collision on the main A road, up near Farm Mere. High-impact collision between bus and motorcycle; potential head injury. Police are already on scene controlling the site.'

If the police had cleared the area, she might

even be able to land on the road. Running through her checks, Piper started the heli up.

'Everybody ready?'

Quickly, the crew ran through their own checks before Piper adjusted her headset and contacted the local air traffic control.

'Heathston Tower, this is Helimed hotel one-niner,' she identified herself. 'We have four on board and we're ready for lift. We're heading about thirty miles north to Farm Mere, following the line of main A road, over.'

And it was strange how, if these were to be her last two weeks for shouts with this crew, she already felt as though she was going to miss it.

'I think the best bet is going to be to RSI him,' Linc decided, less than twenty minutes later as he and his team finished their assessment of the casualty.

It had turned out to be a twenty-five-year-old male who had been heading down the main road when the bus driver, blinded by the sun at the rider's back, had pulled out in front of him.

The young man's body seemed to have borne the brunt of impact, with a broken rib and an open fracture to his lower limb, but it was the potential head injury that was concerning Linc the most.

'Gary was heading to his girlfriend's to propose,' the young man's mother sobbed, having arrived on scene a few minutes earlier, along with the land ambulance crew. 'He said when you know, you know, right?'

'Of course.' Linc nodded empathetically, not prepared for the image of Piper that flashed, unbidden, in his brain.

He thrust it aside.

'So, we've carried out a physical examination, and, along with Gary's agitation and lack of awareness, we're concerned he may have a brain bleed,' Linc informed her, as simply as he could. 'We want to put him into an induced coma to help protect his brain until we can get him to hospital, okay?'

He didn't add that the decision to RSI the woman's son hadn't been taken lightly. His crew knew that timings would be critical, first administering a strong induction agent to sedate him, and swiftly following it up with a rapid-acting paralytic agent in order to both induce unconsciousness and allow them to intubate.

'What do you think he weighs?' Linc asked Tom. 'About eighty kilos?'

'Yeah, I'd say eighty, maybe eighty-five,' Tom agreed as they considered the levels of drugs they needed to administer.

'Okay, Probie, let's run through the checklist,' Linc instructed. 'Then, Tom, you sedate, and we'll bag him for a minute to let that take effect, before administering the next.'

The team worked systematically, running through

the list, and taking advantage of the road ambulance crew who were now also on the ground.

Ten minutes later the team were loading the patient into the heli, with Tom calling it in to the hospital before they set off on the flight. They'd dealt with the lad's other injuries as quickly as they could, but the main focus was still on the brain bleed and trying to stop Gary's brain from swelling.

For the duration of the flight, Linc knew he was going to have to focus primarily on keeping his patient's oxygen and carbon dioxide levels stable.

And still, the mother's comment was floating around Linc's head. *When you know, you know, right?*

Linc wondered if that was true.

Then he wondered why he cared if it was or wasn't.

He was still wondering about it several hours later as his own motorbike hugged the lanes, taking him home after the shift. And most of the evening, as he paced his unexpectedly quiet penthouse. Which felt ridiculously quiet and empty, without Piper's soft voice, or her laugh, which reminded him of a hundred twinkling Christmas lights.

Before Linc realised what he was doing, he picked up his phone and flicked the screen to her number, his thumb hovering over the call button before reason got control of him.

What was he even doing? Had he really been about to call her to find out where she was and if she was okay? Like the kind of boyfriend he definitely wasn't, had *never* been. What had got into him?

It had to be the unexpected news that Albert was on the mend and would be returning sooner, rather than later. News that should delight him. In one way, it did. He was unquestionably relieved for his old buddy that the accident had turned out to be less serious than first imagined, and pleased for Albert that he would be ready to return to the field so relatively quickly.

But at the same time, his thoughts had leapt straight to Piper, and something in his ribcage kicked hard at the idea of her leaving. At never seeing her again. It didn't seem to matter how many times he told himself that she was simply an old friend, or that her leaving his life again had been inevitable.

Even welcome.

It didn't feel very welcome now, knowing that once she returned to barracks, it could be another five years—another fifteen—before he saw her again.

Most likely, it would be a lifetime. And he ought to be fine with that. So why wasn't he?

Why did his body feel as though it were going to implode with the things he was keeping inside?

Piper had been the only person outside his siblings who he'd ever told so much about himself. And even then, it was all he could do not to share the darkest, most damaging secrets of all.

If he wasn't careful, this pent-up sensation was going to swallow him whole. He needed to expend it in some way—he didn't care how.

Stalking down the hallway to his home gym, and hauling off his T-shirt as he went, Linc flicked on the music, letting the low reverb of the bass fill his head. Maybe it could drown out any unwanted voices, needling otherwise.

He had no idea how long he stayed. At least long enough until his hand ached despite the gloves, the sweat was running rivers down his back, and his lungs burned with the effort of breathing.

He was nearing the end of the boxing session when Piper walked in unexpectedly, and, though there was nothing overtly sexual in her attire, his gaze went almost of its own volition to admire the way her jeans clung so lovingly to her backside. He promptly felt like a jerk as she launched into conversation without preamble.

With a low growl of frustration, he turned his attention fully back to the leather bag that had already been bearing the brunt of his confusion—and imagined himself. As though he thought he could wallop some sense into his own head.

'I didn't realise you were home already.' Piper faltered. 'I've been waiting for you in the living room ever since I got back.'

Jab.

'I came straight here.'

Jab, hook.

'I wanted to talk about Albert's return,' she began, before adding hastily, 'Which is great news, of course.'

Abandoning the punchbag, Linc moved quickly to the speed ball. Anything to distract his head and his heart. The rhythm was almost hypnotic, the familiar *thwack-thunk* quickly gathering pace and helping to keep some distance between him and Piper.

His personal best had long been about three hundred and five hits in a minute, but right now he was fairly sure he could easily smash that.

It wasn't something he thought he ought to feel proud about.

'Linc, please,' she blurted out abruptly. 'Stop. Just talk to me.'

The worst of it was that he simply obeyed. Catching the ball with one hand, he turned slowly to face her.

'What do you want to hear, Legs?' he ground out. 'That's it's okay to be upset about your job without anyone accusing you of not being happy Albert's recovering well?'

And he hated himself for the guilt that skittered over her face.

'Of course I'm happy for Albert.'

'As am I.'

When you know, you know, right?

He shook his head free of the echoes.

'I…have a proposal for you,' Piper bit out, on an awkward breath.

And Linc told himself there was no reason that his body should react to that, at all.

'I'm listening,' he told her solemnly instead.

'You remember that I told you I was going for a role at the air ambulance over the border in the next county?'

'West Nessleton Helimed,' he agreed. 'I remember.'

'I understand they already have their go-to list for pilots but what if I agreed to play the part of your date, in exchange for you putting in a good word up there for me? Just to get me an interview, nothing more.'

'You're negotiating with me?' Linc asked, and it was on the tip of his tongue to tell her that he'd already mentioned her name when the regional coordinator had called him a couple of weekends earlier—but something stopped him.

He suspected he knew exactly what that *something* was.

'Yes.' She bobbed her head. 'You need someone

for your sister's wedding, and I need someone to give me a recommendation.'

He ought to say *no*. He ought to walk away. But he found that he couldn't. Faking a date might have seemed like a bad idea when his sister had suggested it but now that Piper was offering to be that date, he found he was suddenly considering it. As insane as it was.

'It isn't a game, Piper,' he growled. 'We'd be staging a relationship, a new side of me.'

'Which you told me last night would buy your brother enough time to convince the wavering board members that the direction he wanted to take the company in is the right one.'

'It would,' Linc confirmed. 'He has several lucrative contracts lined up—they're with the solicitors now but Raf won't rush them. He wants to dot the proverbial "i"s and cross the "t"s. He's thorough—it's what makes him so good at what he does.'

'But the board votes before that, yes?' she pressed. 'So you give the board something to think about and that buys him enough time.'

'In a nutshell,' Linc agreed. 'But using you to convince them I'm ready to change my life? Do I need to remind you of what happened between us the other night?'

Piper twisted her hands in front of her body.

'That was the other night. We were caught off guard and we let things get away from us,' she muttered. And he wondered which of them she was trying to convince more. 'But we've dealt with that now. It's no longer an issue.'

'Isn't it?' he muttered, fighting the pressing urge to take a step forward and reach out his hand to roll a lock of her hair between his fingers.

And when that delicious heat bloomed across her silken skin, he actually *ached* to press his mouth to it.

'It isn't. Like you said, this is a negotiation, nothing more. We both have something the other needs and if we handle it right, then we can both win. West Nessleton is near my family, I couldn't land a better role. But that job opportunity won't be out there for me for ever. So please think about it, Linc. Just don't think too long.'

And then she disappeared through the door and down the hall to her suite. But only because she didn't trust herself with him if she'd stayed in the gym.

He knew, because he didn't trust himself with her either. Not when he suspected that he only had to pull her to him and begin kissing her again for them both to go up in flames.

And *that*, he told himself firmly, would not be a good idea for anyone.

CHAPTER TEN

WHEN HE'D SAID the family home, Piper realised a few days later as they were flown over the countryside in the family's private helicopter, what he'd really meant was *ancestral* home.

With hindsight, she shouldn't have expected anything less than the vast, sprawling country pile with land surrounding it in all directions.

'This is where you grew up?' Piper couldn't help but gape as she shifted in one of the oversized, butter-soft seats. 'How far does it extend?'

Without warning, Linc leaned closer to her, to place his eyeline approximately around hers. The effect on Piper was instantaneous, making her hot and jittery. And her skin seemed to pull so tight, almost as if it were suddenly too small for her own body.

'See that treeline over there, by the stone church?'

She wasn't sure how long it took her to remember to breathe.

'I...yes.'

'To the shoreline down there?' He swept his arm across the other way, where Piper could see the sea in the near distance.

'Right.' She swallowed. Hard.

'And then from that winding country lane that bisects the county up there, down to the golf course over there.'

'I guess it's some people's dream to live next to a golf course,' she managed, her voice sounding thicker than usual.

'In the interests of full disclosure, the golf course belongs to us. Stoneywell Golf Course—it hosts some of the top annual gold tournaments.'

'Of course,' she choked out, but that could hardly be helped.

Just another thing to add to the fact that the area he'd indicated had to be hundreds upon hundreds of hectares. The entire housing estate where she'd grown up could have fitted into his mere back garden, several times over. Linc came from an entirely different world from the one she'd come from, and that gap between the two of them couldn't have been more striking.

Or humiliating.

For the first time, something slid down her back. Perhaps it was apprehension, more likely it was resignation. Just another place she didn't really fit in—no matter how much she might try to tell herself otherwise. Pretending to be Linc's fiancé in exchange for his good word was one thing. But what if someone got curious about her? Or worse, recognised her?

'It is,' Linc's voice came back over the headset as he dipped his head in acknowledgement. It left her scrambling to remember what her question had even been.

And still, she couldn't seem to stop her tongue from moving.

'Say again?'

'You asked if this was where I grew up,' he reminded her. 'And it is. It's where Raf and I climbed trees and built forest dens. It's where we learned to shoot clay pigeons, and fish, and ride.'

'You ride?'

Of course he would do, coming from a place like this, she realised belatedly.

'Not as much as I'd like to, any more. Though I used to love it. Raf and I often took our horses down to the beach and then galloped on the sand. You've never ridden?'

'Never.' She shook her head.

'Not even on holiday?'

'Not even donkey rides on the beach.' Her smile was rueful.

A part of her had dreamed of it, as a kid. But when she was growing up, her family had never had that kind of money. Not even before all the financial worries.

'I'll teach you. It's easy enough.'

She seriously doubted that, though she didn't say as much. What was Linc doing anyway, suggesting things like that? They both knew she was only here for the wedding rehearsal dinner, definitely not long enough for her to do anything like learning to ride a horse.

For the next few moments, she sat in silence, drinking it all in as the pilot brought their luxury heli down onto the estate's bespoke helipad. Just like another parking bay, to a place like this.

What she wasn't particularly expecting was the welcoming party that appeared to be waiting for them near what had to be an imposing eight-foot-high wooden front door. Linc's sister, of course, along with who was likely her fiancé. And Raf—as tall, dark, and brooding as before. Today the fraternal resemblance seemed all the more striking.

Then, before she knew what was happening, the heli was down, the engine off and the blades stopped, and Linc was out of the aircraft and reaching back to help her down. Under other circumstances, she felt she would have brushed away his unnecessarily chivalrous offer, but now it was all Piper could do to release his hand once her feet were firmly on land.

The welcoming party swept forward, and she noted that Sara's fiancé appeared to have slipped away as they'd landed.

'Lincoln.' Sara smiled, hugging him quickly before turning to her. 'And... Piper. It's nice to meet you again.'

The steely smile was still there...just decidedly more polished. Presumably under threat from either Linc, or Raf. Possibly both. Even so, Piper felt her mind go blank and just as she was about to wish she'd never agreed to do this she felt Linc's warm hand brush the small of her back, silently lending her strength.

She discreetly drew in as steadying a breath as she could and turned to Linc's sister.

'Lady Sara,' she managed politely, before turning to Linc's brother. 'Lord Ranulph.'

'Sara and Raf will be fine,' Linc stopped her tightly. 'Isn't that right, Sara?'

'As you're our brother's guest, we don't stand on formality,' Raf's rich, deep, familiar-sounding voice agreed smoothly. 'It's very good to meet you again, Piper. We're grateful to you for persuading my brother here to finally return home.'

Raf held out his hand to shake hers, and the severe expression on his face gave way to that surprisingly warm, equally familiar smile. And once again Piper was struck by the connection between the two brothers. That kind of easiness; a bond. A trust.

It made Piper want to trust Raf, too.

'Isn't that so, Sara?'

'Raf…' This time the interjection earned her a withering look from her older brother.

'Would you care to address Linc's guest as Captain Green for the duration of her stay?' the older brother asked quietly. Firmly.

'She isn't serving any more,' Linc's sister objected for a moment, before appearing to bite her tongue. 'Fine.' She flashed a tight smile, though it was clear she didn't like it.

'Piper acting as my fiancée was your idea, after all.' Linc finally deigned to speak but made no attempt to conceal the amusement in his tone.

'You having a date was my idea,' his sister snapped. 'This engagement twist was all your idea. Be it on your heads when people ask you all about your relationship and you can't answer.'

'And therein lies the fun.'

Sara cast him a withering glower.

'That's always been your problem, Lincoln, you treat everything like a game.'

Linc slung his bag over his shoulder, his hand returning to the small of Piper's back. 'Shall we find our rooms?'

Strong, comforting, and more than a little welcome.

'Linc, if you have a moment.' His brother moved to walk beside them, his hands clasped behind his back, back to serious mode again. 'There have been a couple of recent developments with the board.'

'You want to talk about them now?' Linc asked, his deep voice matching the calm gravity of his brother's.

'Not this moment, but as soon as you get chance.'

'You ought to know about them,' Sara noted

pointedly. 'The sooner the better. I can show your guest to the suite.'

'I think not,' he declined, moving to walk with her.

And she could accept it gratefully or do what she was supposed to be here to do.

'I'll be fine,' Piper told him quickly, before she could bottle out.

'I thought we could take a walk together.' He leaned in so that only she could hear, the soft sweep of his breath at her neck making her shiver with delight before she could stop herself. 'Perhaps escape this place.'

'I'd like that,' she murmured back. 'As soon as you're finished with Raf and Sara.'

'Piper…'

'Truly,' she managed firmly.

Linc eyed her wordlessly, then he looked at his brother. Finally he dipped his head and fell in beside his brother, the two of them walking with their heads bowed together. And Piper couldn't help but notice Sara staring wistfully after them as they went. The younger sister who might have spent her whole life racing to catch up with her two, bigger brothers.

Piper couldn't explain why she had to fight back the wealth of emotions rioting through her at that moment. Perhaps because it made her think of her own family—her own sister—and the ugliness that had marred their relationship ever since before their father had died.

Seeing Linc's interplay with his family—both the other night, and now—had been unexpected… and unsettling. In an instant, she'd been able to imagine exactly what the trio must have been like as kids. A tight little band of three, growing up in a place like Oakenfeld Hall.

It had her revisiting all her military memories of Linc, seeing them in a new light. Raf the older one, always trying to be responsible and keep the peace. Sara was the baby of the group, the daughter torn between living up to her title as a lady, and wanting to tomboy it around with big brothers who she clearly idolised.

As for Linc, he was the middle kid. The second brother who would neither be the heir to the dukedom, nor the much-vaunted daughter. No wonder he'd carved out his own place in the world by joining the army, and becoming a doctor.

Could it be that his enigmatic personality was less about keeping others out, and more about protecting himself? Piper stared at Linc for a moment, her mind reeling.

'Can I ask you something?'

Piper swivelled around in surprise as Sara fell in beside her. And even though it was phrased as a question, there was a peremptory tone to Sara's voice that brooked little argument. The customs of being a lady who commanded attention, Piper presumed.

Still, she forced another smile, for Linc's sake.

'Of course. I'll try to answer if I can.'

'Why are you doing this?'

She didn't need to elaborate for Piper to know what she meant. For a moment, she wondered whether she should stick with the old army buddies connection, but there was something too practical about Sara for that to satisfy her. In the end, Piper plumped for the truth.

Or a part-truth, at least.

'I'm leaving the Army Air Corps. We agreed that if I attend this weekend's rehearsal dinner and next week's wedding as his fiancée, then he'll recommend me as pilot for one of the other air ambulance bases.'

'One of the other air ambulance bases?'

'In the next county.'

Sara cast her an assessing glance.

'Why not the one where you both are now?'

'Heathston already has Albert.' No need to tell Sara that he was retiring. 'Besides, my mother and brother live a county over. The other base will let me be nearer to them.'

'You're moving to be closer to your family?' Sara eyed her even more intently. 'How old is your brother?'

'He's twelve,' Piper couldn't help but smile.

'Sometimes twelve going on forty, other times twelve going on about seven.'

'So family is important to you?' Linc's sister didn't even crack a smile, but there was an earnest note to her voice that hadn't been there before.

'It is,' Piper answered after a moment. 'Even when I was away, I used to speak to them as often as I could. They're all I have.'

'Just like Raf and Linc are all I have now. And my future husband, of course.'

'Of course.' Piper kept her voice light.

'It's why I want Linc to come home. We need him here. He belongs back here.'

'He doesn't belong in a clinic.' The words tumbled softly from Piper's lips before she could stop herself. Before her brain could engage. 'He's an army doctor, or an air ambulance doctor, getting out there to the patient and saving lives in the field. I don't think Linc would ever be a good wait-for-them-to-come-to-him kind of doctor.'

Instantly, she realised her mistake. She braced herself, waiting for some cold dismissal from Linc's fierce sister. Sara might have engaged in this conversation with her, but, for Linc's sake, she should have thought twice about saying something that would agitate the bride-to-be.

'That's pretty much what Linc said the other night.' The sad admission shocked Piper.

And even though she knew she shouldn't press her luck, she heard herself speaking again.

'For what it's worth, it's always been evident that Linc loves you and your brother very much. I think a part of him would even want to return home. I just think…there's a barrier there, and I don't know why but he can't seem to overcome it.'

Slamming her mouth shut, Piper braced again. There was no question this time that Sara would think she had overstepped her boundaries.

Yet, once again, Linc's sister shocked her.

'Do you…?' She tailed off, shaking her head. And then, 'Do you think he wants to, though? Overcome that barrier, I mean?'

'I don't know,' Piper told her truthfully. 'I don't know the full story, clearly—Linc has never shared that. But… I think so.'

Sara nodded. And then, as if she hadn't shocked Piper enough already, she drew in a deep breath.

'I think, perhaps, I have misjudged you,' she managed, awkwardly. As if she wasn't accustomed to having to make such admissions. 'Perhaps you're not such a poor decision by my brother, after all. We shall see.'

Then, as though putting an end to the exchange, Sara lifted her head and picked up the pace as they hurried to the great staircase. All Piper could do was follow.

'Is this walk so that I can escape this place?' Piper asked wryly as she followed him through a door off the long, elegant hallway. 'Or so that you can?'

'Perhaps a little of both,' he admitted grudgingly, leading her down a tight, winding staircase, and through a low door. 'I have a confession to make, Piper. You don't need to be here.'

'I don't?'

'I talked to Regional about you weeks ago—the moment I heard about the pilot opening at West Nessleton. So you don't need to be here.'

'I don't understand.' Her brow furrowed in confusion. 'You don't *want* me here?'

'I'm saying you don't *have* to be. I know how overbearing Sara can be, not to mention the people who'll be watching us this weekend, scrutinising us, and looking for any weakness.'

'Did your brother say something?' she asked, without thinking.

Still, she wasn't prepared for Linc to look so sheepish.

'He may have reminded me what I was about to subject you to between extended family and the board. I wanted to give you one last chance to back out.'

And Piper thought it was that moment that made her all the more determined to stay and help him out. Smiling to herself, she glanced around at the scenery, then pulled up short.

'Wait, are these the kitchen gardens? They're beautiful.'

She stopped to take a better look around, pleased when Linc moved to stand next to her.

'They were designed by my great-great-great-grandmother in eighteen seventy, and re-imagined by my father and grandfather before Raf was even born. Over there, you can see fig trees and apple trees, and over that way are grapevines.'

She followed his hand, taking in the rich display.

'And if you look this way—' he placed his hands on her shoulders to turn her as she pretended not to notice the shiver of pleasure that danced along her spine '—you can find prickly cucumbers and even liquorice.'

'Is this where you spent time with your father?'

He turned back sharply.

'What made you ask that?'

Piper shrugged. The question had been out before she'd even realised she'd intended to ask it.

'I don't know, you just love cooking and you're so passionate about the ingredients you use...' She tailed off.

But just as she thought Linc was going to ignore her and start walking again, he surprised her.

'Yeah, I guess it is where my father and I bonded most. Here, pottering around the gardens in the precious little time he got to spend here, or riding across the fields.'

'But here was more special?' she guessed. 'Because riding was with your siblings, and the garden was just you and him?'

Another pause.

'The garden was just for the two of us,' Linc agreed at length. 'And a couple of gardeners, of course. Now it's just the gardeners, and we run culinary courses from the estate; the guests get to choose their ingredients from everything that we grow.'

They stood, quietly watching, for a few more moments before Linc seemed to take in a deep breath, and strode forward.

'Come on, there's plenty more to show you.'

For the next couple of hours, Piper let Linc take her around his childhood home, showing her everywhere from the formal gardens where the public were allowed to admire the house, to the private grove of trees where he and his siblings first learned to climb.

She walked the light trail with him, imagining how pretty the stone bridge must look at night, strewn with colourful lights that twinkled and shimmered in the reflection of the water beneath.

And then, suddenly, they were down by the sea; on the private stretch of beach that belonged to the family.

'I don't understand why Sara doesn't just get married in some private ceremony here on the beach, instead of some spectacle with a couple of hundred guests we barely even know, let alone like.'

Piper blinked, and she despaired of herself for

the butterflies that were now fluttering madly—unfittingly—around her stomach.

Grimly, she attempted to quash them.

'Is that why you're so against your brother-in-law? Because he's agreeing to what you'd call a *spectacle* of a wedding?'

'I'd rather he asked her to scale everything back. I think that might take some of this unnecessary pressure off her. Duke's daughter or not, there's no need for all the fanfare. I can't help wondering if he's encouraging Sara because of how good it could make *him* look.'

'Have you asked your sister?'

Linc didn't answer immediately, instead choosing to glower out to sea—and at the bright sunlight as it glanced off the cold waves.

Piper wrinkled her nose and tried again.

'Sara doesn't seem the type to let herself get pushed into something she doesn't want.'

'You'd be surprised,' Linc replied darkly. 'She has always demanded more of herself than anyone else ever did. I suspect she might think a lavish wedding is her way of supporting Raf.'

'Why?'

'I don't know. As a reminder of how much weight the Stoneywell name holds?'

It was so far removed from Piper's own reality that she was almost frightened to answer and show herself up.

'The point is,' he continued, when she didn't answer, 'that it isn't just about me not seeing why she needs all this fuss or fanfare. It's more that I don't even understand why she's getting married at all.'

'Perhaps because she loves her fiancé?'

Piper tried to keep her voice upbeat but there was no mistaking the strain in her voice. After the way her father had treated her mother, she wasn't sure she believed in love either.

Wasn't it just a way to get away with treating another person as if they were dirt?

'You don't believe in real love any more than I do, Legs.' Linc snorted humourlessly, as if reading her mind. 'You act happy for couples, but I know how much we both wonder what the hell they're thinking of, tying themselves to another person for life.'

'I don't think that,' Piper objected. Weakly.

He shook his head.

'You might fool others, but you forget how long we've known each other. I've seen your expression when buddies gave up their military careers for their new spouse, the disbelief. Something you couldn't quite understand because you never would have done that. Neither would I. You and I are the same.'

'I gave up flying army helicopters for the love of my family,' she pointed out, but the nose wrinkle gave her away.

'Did you?' he challenged. 'Or was your reason

more practical? Did you actually have much of a choice?'

She didn't answer him. She didn't need to.

'The same as I did,' he carried on after a moment. 'The only reason I gave up my army medical career was because of that final ambush. Because I have responsibilities within this family, and because my father's ill health meant that Raf was fighting avaricious board members. At that time, he couldn't have held them off whilst Sara and I were living the lives we were living.

'You were an army doctor.' Piper frowned. 'What's so damaging about that?'

'Nothing, in itself.'

But the dark look that stole across his taut expression told a different story. Furious yet lost, all at the same time. The two emotions seemed to war across his features, then stole inside her ribcage like a fist, and squeezed. And then squeezed some more.

'Linc?' she prompted, unable to help herself.

'It's a story you don't want to hear, Piper.'

She didn't understand what made her close the gap between them. Or what made her reach up and place her palms to his chest. But suddenly, there she was. More than that, he wasn't pulling away.

'Try me,' she whispered. 'Why do you seem to be carrying such guilt around with you, Linc? What is it that you feel you owe your siblings?'

And she wasn't sure how long they stood there—perhaps whole lifetimes—and Piper pulled her lips into a tight, nervous line as she tried to will him not to shut her out, the way he always seemed to shut everyone out.

But even as she knew that was exactly what he was doing, preparing to push her away, a movement across the landscape caught her attention. A figure swaying oddly.

She watched in horror as the man suddenly buckled, then collapsed to the floor.

'Linc…' she cried instinctively. 'Over there.'

CHAPTER ELEVEN

VAULTING THE WALL, not needing to look to know that Piper would be following, Linc raced across the fairway and to the men.

He was almost grateful for the distraction. There was no way he had been prepared to answer Piper's questions.

Even as he ran he noted the two figures hunched over a third. It certainly looked as if they were attempting chest compressions but the rhythm was wrong. Too slow. And the closer he got, the more he could see it looked like two guys in their twenties over a likely fifty-something bloke.

'Is he okay? Can I help?'

The two men cranked their heads to him in evident relief.

'It's our dad. We think he's had a heart attack,' one of them—the older-looking one who was attempting chest compressions—managed in a strangled voice.

'Can you do that CPR thing?' The other looked up at them helplessly.

'I can. I'm a doctor,' Linc assured them as he dropped beside the collapsed man and checked for breathing or a pulse. The man had neither. 'Can you tell me what happened?'

The two sons eyed him, somewhat stunned, before the older one spoke again.

'He said he was feeling a little bit faint, and then he just…collapsed.'

'Any history of illness?' Linc pressed.

'No.' The two men looked at each other before shaking their heads. 'Nothing.'

'Have you called emergency services?'

Again the two men looked blankly at each other.

'We were more concerned with doing CPR. I mean, that was the right thing to do, wasn't it?'

'Exactly right,' Linc assured them. 'You did well, and now we're here to help. Piper, can you—?'

'Already on it,' she confirmed as her mobile connected to the emergency services, stepping to one side to deal with them whilst Linc continued the chest compressions.

They both knew the odds on a person surviving a heart attack outside a hospital were low— around ten per cent, according to heart charity figures. But it didn't mean he wasn't about to do his damnedest to make this the *one*. It was what he was programmed to do.

'Right, I'll do the compressions.' He looked at the calmer of the two brothers, then indicated to the ground on the other side of their father. 'You can kneel here and ensure his airway remains clear.'

'The clubhouse has a defib,' the other brother remembered suddenly. 'Should I call them?'

Linc nodded.

'Yes, call them. Tell them that your father is in cardiac arrest, and to bring any other kit they have.'

'I'll help.' Piper stepped back to the group. 'The land ambulance is on its way.'

'Acknowledged.'

With one ear to the boys, and the rest of his focus on the man on the ground in front of him, Linc realised it was good to realise that one person he wasn't worried about was Piper. If anything, her presence could only make the entire scenario that much easier.

It was more than he could say for any other date he might have chosen to bring to this damned wedding.

For the next few minutes Linc worked with one of the sons to keep the blood and oxygen flowing around their father's body, surprised when Piper returned so quickly with the medical kit.

'They were already on their way,' Piper told him quickly. 'Another player had seen him collapse and alerted the clubhouse.'

'Right, can you take over chest compressions whilst I set it out?'

She hurried around to drop by his side, already in place to minimise time off the chest, as Linc made way for her, counting out her rhythm before he'd even got to his feet.

Quickly, he took a pair of scissors from the kit and cut the man's clothing away to give them better access.

'Okay, machine is charging.' He announced his warning a minute or so later, having set everything up. 'And stand clear.'

As the machine gave its warning sounds, Piper lifted her hands off the man's chest, moving backwards.

'Rhythm check,' Linc announced, bending down to check for a pulse. There was nothing.

'No.' Piper shook her head, also checking the femoral, as the defib machine reported its own automatic results.

'No output PEA,' Linc confirmed. 'Continue CPR.'

Wordlessly, Piper resumed compressions. Another couple of minutes and they could try shocking the patient again. The bleeping and automatic instruction from the defib machine rolled around them, but it was Linc's presence that was giving her the most confidence.

'Machine charging,' he warned again, a few moments later as the defib bleeped. 'Off the chest, and clear.'

Another shock. Another check.

'Rhythm check?' He had nothing.

Piper began to shake her head, then hesitated.

'I think they can feel a beat.'

Linc moved to her position and made a check of his own. It was faint, but there was something there.

'Let's continue CPR,' he said. 'Do you want a break?'

'Okay for now,' she confirmed, bracing her arms and beginning another strong set, leaving him free to carry out his other checks.

By the time the land ambulance turned up about five minutes later, the man's heart was beating again.

'He's making some respiratory effort,' Linc told them as he handed over. 'You'll want to intubate to minimise damage to the brain, as well as give him some medication to help blow off the carbon dioxide build-up.'

With both teams working together, it wasn't too long before the man was on a scoop and in the ambulance, his chances looking far more promising than they had done less than half an hour earlier.

And as they watched the ambulance roll off the fairway and back to the main road, Linc couldn't help thinking how easy everything was with Piper around. Not just the way she had slotted in to help, even though she was usually the pilot, not the paramedic, but the way she'd slotted in here with his family. Into his life.

It was the same way she'd been out on tour all

those years ago. That same quiet confidence that had attracted him to her back then.

But that still didn't explain why he'd almost decided to open himself up to her the way he had done, down on the beach earlier. Why he was ready to reveal secrets to her that he had never even shared with his sister. Or fully explored with Raf.

What was it about Piper Green that had him turning inside out? Worse, he wasn't even sure that he minded.

Piper watched the land ambulance roll carefully off the fairway, hoping that everything they'd just done would be enough to save their impromptu patient's life.

But her mind was already shifting back to the man beside her. The man who, if she wasn't very much mistaken, had been about to shut her down the way she was beginning to realise he always did. Only now, he was looking at her with a different expression on his face. One that was familiar, and unfamiliar, all at the same time.

'You asked me what is it that I feel I owe my siblings,' he repeated without warning, and when his gaze slid to hers she refused to look away.

'I did,' she agreed softly. 'Anyone who watches the three of you together can see the love and respect you all share, so why have you built this wall between them and you? Do you begrudge your sister's wedding so much?'

It wasn't even a guess. It was more words that flitted through her head and out of her mouth, trying to find some button, some trigger, that might help him to talk to her.

'I don't begrudge my sister anything,' he bit out defensively.

It wasn't the button she'd been looking for, but it was something. The tiniest wedge, a fraction of a millimetre in an almost non-existent gap. All she had to do was nudge it in that little bit further.

'Then what is it, Linc? Because there's something going on here, and if I'm going to play this part for you all this weekend, then I ought to understand it, at least.'

'There is no *ought* about it,' Linc clipped out. 'But since you're suddenly so damned interested, I'll tell you. My parents never had what you might call a good marriage—no great shock there, plenty of couples don't—but as the Duke and Duchess of Stoneywell, divorce was never on the cards. Lady Oakes, the Duchess of Stoneywell, you surely know the name, Piper?'

Even as she shook her head to deny it, something shifted in the recesses of her brain. An old story she hadn't heard since she was a kid.

'The Duchess of Stoneywell... Lady Oakes.' Piper's brow furrowed deeply. 'I think I know those names.'

'I imagine you do.' It was all he could do to keep his mouth from twisting up in disgust. 'She was nothing if not attention-hungry, our mother. If she wasn't centre of attention then she wasn't happy, and if she wasn't happy then no one else could be, either.'

Piper wanted to answer. She wanted to say something to help, but nothing would. So she stayed silent, and simply listened.

'No matter that our father was trying to be the duke and run a demanding estate, and keep a business afloat in a harsh economic climate so that hundreds of employees didn't lose their jobs—my mother wanted more of his time. His attention. Not because she loved him, you understand, but because she was a narcissist and couldn't stand the idea that not everything revolved around her.

'And when she didn't get the duke's attention— she looked elsewhere for her fun. Worse, she made sure everyone knew how overlooked and unappreciated she was, and how her husband didn't make time for her. She told anyone who would listen how unkind he was to her. Emotional cruelty, I believe she told one paper.'

So that was why Linc had never courted attention, Piper realised suddenly. It was why he didn't want publicity, and had never told anyone in the army, or in the air ambulance, who he really was. It was beginning to make sense now.

And crazily—dangerously—it made Piper feel special that she was the one he was confiding in.

'My father was always blinded by my mother. She was his downfall from the start. She wanted money, and to live the life of a duchess, but she didn't want any of the responsibility. She hated my father for being so upright, and moral, and boring.'

'I don't understand.'

'My mother brought scandal after scandal to the family—in fact, she was a scandal all to herself. The revelation that I was a bastard son was just her final coup de grâce. Raf and I only realised recently how much our father protected our family from her indiscretions—even up until her death. The papers had run stories about her from time to time, over the years—from deeply unflattering stories, to downright disgusting rumours. I'm surprised you didn't read any of them. She certainly did her best to get them into every media outlet going if it increased her exposure—in more ways than one.'

Piper squinted, fervently trying to recollect vague memories. She'd never really been one for gossip columns, or glossy mag tell-alls. Now that Linc had put it into her head, she did think she recalled a few less than pleasant things.

'That was her?'

'That was her.' Linc dipped his head curtly. 'You understand now why I never wanted to bring anyone back here. I didn't want to subject them to this, but also, I didn't want the gossip or the attention. Raf can do well without my name being associated with his.'

She shook her head vehemently.

'You didn't give them anything. Your father knew the truth and he didn't care.'

'Our mother did our best to drag our family through the mud, whilst our father was fierce about protecting the three of us from all of it.'

'Your father sounds like a decent, upstanding gentleman.'

'He was,' Linc managed fiercely. 'He stood up for what he believed in, and what he thought was right, and damn the rest of it. I'll never match him. Not like Raf does. I'm my mother's son, but I'm not his son.'

The roaring started in her brain in an instant, at the mention of scandal. As though she feared her own life might seep into his. She thrust it aside. That wasn't going to happen. Here she was telling Linc not to let his past and his mother's sins ruin his relationship with his siblings, and she was about to let her own past, and her father's sins, ruin this moment with Linc.

It was too much for either of them to have to bear.

'These aren't your sins to bear, Linc,' Piper said softly, realising that her words were as much for herself as for him. 'Your father never thought they were, and your siblings certainly don't. Raf and

Sara are asking for your help because it's their ex-cuse to get you back home. They aren't holding you accountable, you must see that.'

'They don't need to hold me accountable, Legs. I hold myself accountable.'

'Is that why you've built this invisible wall be-tween them and you? Is that why you keep them at arm's length? Why you joined the army? The only reason your sister keeps pushing you towards the Stoneywell Medical Centre is because it's the only thing she can think of to bring you back home.'

'It isn't for me,' Linc growled, but it wasn't as fierce as before.

She was getting through to him, and for some reason that made her feel good. More than good.

'And she knows that, but she tries anyway be-cause she wants her brother back in her life. They both do.'

'Our lives aren't compatible.' Linc refused to agree, as Piper splayed her hand over his ribcage as though that could help her to reach him faster.

'Only if you don't want them to be. There are a hundred things you could do back here, with your medical skill, and as Lord Lincoln, if you wanted to. Like setting up a Stoneywell air ambulance for a start—look at what might have happened today if you and I hadn't been passing that golf course right at that moment.'

'You can pretend scandal goes away all you want to, Piper. But take it from someone who knows, the truth is that it never does. It follows a person, and rears its head at the worst times. No one can escape it. No one ever will.

And later, much later, when the roar had died down in her brain and her heart had stopped hammering around her ribcage, Piper would think it was that precise moment—those precise words— that had felled her at the knees.

Because he'd brought her to the table as a way to help douse any vicious rumours. But if anyone decided to look into her, and expose her own set of sordid truths, then she could do Linc and his family far, far more harm than good.

Her stomach heaved, and lurched. She'd spent so many years trying to bury this truth, from herself as much as anyone else. But now, there was nothing else for it; she needed to tell him the truth. Not now. Not when the rehearsal dinner was this evening.

But after that, perhaps when they left Oakenfeld Hall and went back to his penthouse. Certainly before the wedding next week.

Before someone else lit the match and it all went up in flames.

Taking both of them with it.

CHAPTER TWELVE

THE WOMAN WAS a damned enchantress.

Linc watched Piper shimmer and charm her way around the room—just as he'd known that she would. Just as she'd always been able to handle herself around brigadiers and generals, and charm their respective spouses.

Just as she'd always charmed him.

It ought to concern him just how easily he felt she slotted into the role as his fiancée—*pretend* fiancée—but he found he was more spellbound than disquieted. And didn't that say something in itself?

Even Raf had remarked how happy he looked, earlier that evening when his brother had walked in to find him retrieving his grandmother's jewels from the study safe to lend to Piper. And when he'd pre-empted Raf's objection to lending out their grandmother's ruby necklace, reminding his brother—and possibly himself—that it was all just a ploy, he thought it was telling that Raf's only response had been, 'At least one of us should be happy.'

As though it were real.

It didn't help that Piper's words were still stalking around his brain. Could she be right about why he'd stayed away all this time—with the army, and now as a Helimed doctor? She made him question whether he had really been helping his family the way he'd once told himself he was doing.

Not that he was about to give up being a doctor. But perhaps moving a little closer to home might not be the worst idea, after all.

And Piper?

Ignoring the question, Linc set down his brandy tumbler onto the bar top, so loudly that the ice cubes rattled, and swung around so that his back was completely to the woman who seemed to occupy more of his thoughts than ever.

It didn't work.

Moments later, Linc found himself striding across the floor and towards her, before he even realised what he intended.

'Dance?' he bit out, less a suggestion and more an order, as he held his hand out.

And he had to fight to pretend not to notice the current of electricity that jolted through him, when she reached out obligingly, and slipped her smaller hand into his.

Without a word, he led her to the floor, before sweeping her into his arms for a simple waltz. And, just like that, the rest of the room—the rest of the world—fell away, and Piper was all he could see. All he could smell—from the pleasant citrus notes of her shampoo to that delicate note of her perfume.

His entire body prickled with awareness—and not just the more obvious, baser parts of his anatomy. Had any woman before ever affected him the way that Piper did? Pretend relationship or not, he was terribly afraid he knew the answer to that.

'Was my role not to mingle whilst you talked to board members and let them think you were ready to return home to the family fold?' she murmured up at him.

Though he noticed even as they danced that she seemed as incapable of tearing her gaze from him as he was of looking away from her. Linc took that as a positive.

'It was indeed.' He lowered his mouth closer to her ear, telling himself it was so that no one could possibly overhear their conversation. 'I understand we've already given them a great deal to mull over.'

'Oh?'

'I'm told that those who were arguing for my shares to be stripped from me, and who were using this evening as an opportunity to put forward their case, are now beginning to lose their collective voice.'

'That's good news, isn't it?'

Was he only fooling himself to think that the faint quiver in her voice intensified the closer his lips came to her skin?

'It's very good news,' he agreed. 'What's more, Raf tells me that he has already been approached by several board members who had been wavering before, but who are now ready to throw their full weight behind him. And I'm beginning to wonder if returning home might be a good idea, after all.'

She stiffened in his arms, her feet momentarily faltering. But he held her to him and kept them moving gracefully around the dance floor.

'You're thinking about really leaving Heathston? Not to run a medical centre, surely?'

This time, he knew he didn't imagine the shiver that rippled through Piper.

'And what happens when you don't have a fiancée after all? When you don't get married, or have kids, or all those things they believe a true Oakes lord should do?'

And the odd thing was that Linc couldn't explain why. He had never, not once, imagined himself getting married and having a family. Now, suddenly, he could. The image was distant, and somewhat hazy, but for the first time in his life, it was actually there. The only thing he could make out clearly was Oakenfeld Hall in the background.

Had Piper been right, that being an army doc had been his way of escaping the life to which he'd never quite reconciled himself? And had she also had a point that the day he would find peace would be the day he accepted that he was part of this family whether the duke was his biological father or not?

'What you said today about it being time this

region had a Helimed to service it, that made sense to me.'

Piper blinked at him.

'Well, yes. It would certainly have helped that man today.'

'Perhaps Oakenfeld Hall could sponsor a Helimed team up here. It would be something that would fit with my father's vision for Oakenfeld Industries—giving back to the community.'

'It makes sense,' she agreed, though her unexpectedly taut body was at odds with the sentiment.

'It does. That way I could also attend board meetings. Perhaps it's time I actually supported Raf and Sara and be present at these things.'

What made it so strange was the fact that he actually wanted to. Ten years ago, being back here he'd felt like a cuckoo in the nest. Even five years ago, he hadn't quite...*fitted*. But now, with Piper by his side, it felt somehow...*right*.

Except that Piper wasn't part of the equation. He shouldn't have to keep reminding himself of that fact.

Whatever the hell that was supposed to mean.

'That's great,' she managed, forcing a bright smile that was entirely at odds with the way her body was tensing so strangely in his arms.

Though he told himself he had no intention of saying anything, Linc heard the next suggestion slipping out of his mouth.

'The place would need a pilot. Should you decide West Nessleton Helimed isn't for you.'

'I can't move anywhere.' Piper laughed, though it sounded hollow to his ears. Or perhaps he was merely imagining it. 'My mother and my brother need me.'

He wanted to ask what it was that Piper herself needed. But he stopped himself.

'Of course.' He nodded curtly.

'If it wasn't for them, then maybe…' Her voice sounded thick. Unfamiliar.

But he could hardly process it for the racket going on in his head.

'You don't need to explain yourself,' he growled.

And he assured himself that the uninvited feeling in his chest—which felt altogether too much like regret—was purely because it would be a shame for his new Helimed operation to lose out on a pilot of Piper's calibre.

'Linc, there's something…' The tortured words caught in her throat as she stared at him miserably. A haunted note that reached inside his chest and squeezed. 'There's something I need to tell you.'

'You don't need to say a thing,' he made himself bite back, telling himself he was grateful for the reality check.

He even thought he might believe it himself.

'I do need to.'

And he couldn't tell whether it was the most honest truth she'd ever told him, or a complete lie. Before he realised what he was doing, Linc lowered his head to Piper's ear.

'You should never feel as though you have to do anything.'

'Right,' she muttered, turning her head.

And as their lips brushed each other's, the contact shot through him, demanding more, and making him greedy.

'I think we can do better than that,' he murmured.

Wordlessly, Piper pressed her body tighter against his, and perhaps it was the way her body seemed to mould itself to his, or maybe it was the incredible soft, sweet groan of pleasure she made as he fitted his lips to hers, but an intense heat seared through Linc.

White-hot and gloriously electric—unlike anything he had ever known before.

Because Piper's unlike any woman you've ever known before.

He beat the voice back, but there was no denying the truth in the words.

Piper was perfection. She tasted of longing, and need, and all manner of sinful things that he'd spent the better part of a decade telling himself he didn't imagine every time he'd looked at this woman. From the swell of her breasts pressing against his chest, to the scrape of her tongue against his.

As if they'd both been waiting for this moment

for a lifetime. Even two. Linc forgot that this was all meant to be a show, pretend. He only knew that he didn't want to stop. Didn't think he *could* stop.

He found himself pouring himself into the kiss. Confessing a thousand truths to her that he couldn't say with words—not even in the privacy of his own head.

But they were in that kiss, and he couldn't seem to stem them.

This was the excuse he'd been looking for. The moment to allow them both to cross that invisible line they'd drawn between them in the desert sand, all those years ago. And her presence at this dinner no longer felt pretend, or staged, perhaps it never really had done. It felt right, as though she belonged here, by his side, every bit as much as he did.

The kiss stretched on for ever, glorious and exultant. But when they finally pulled apart, coming up for air and remembering where they were, he knew he wasn't ready to let the evening end with just that.

By the glazed expression in Piper's stunning eyes, and her telltale rapid pulse at her throat—the one that begged him to cover it with his mouth—she felt exactly the same way.

Suddenly the ballroom felt too crowded. Too suffocating. Abruptly, he dropped his arms from around his fake fiancée's luscious body while keeping hold of her hand, then turned her round and ushered them both off the dance floor.

'Where are we going?' she asked breathlessly as they weaved their way through the crowd.

Linc couldn't bring himself to answer. He couldn't bring himself to do anything to break the moment; to give him pause to rethink what he was about to do. What he'd wanted to do with this one woman from the first time he'd ever laid eyes on her, before they'd thrown up obstacles such as *professional behaviour*, and *duty*.

But now none of those obstacles existed any more and finally, *finally*, they could be honest with each other about who they really were. And what they wanted from the other.

Piper allowed Linc to guide her out of the ballroom without another word.

After that earth-shattering kiss, she was finding it hard enough to remember to breathe, let alone talk.

That kiss...

It took everything she had not to lift her fingers to her lips in wonder—just to check that she hadn't been dreaming it.

He'd turned her inside out. In one single kiss, he'd wiped away all the fears that had been racing around her head that evening. Even now, her mind grappled for them but came up empty-handed.

All she could think about was Linc. The kiss

had erased every apprehensive notion she'd ever felt. It had been perfect. They'd fitted together perfectly.

As if they'd been hand-crafted for each other, something inside her whispered.

If he could do that with just one simple kiss, what could he do to her with something more intimate? If she continued walking with him along that corridor and upstairs to the bedroom—where he was patently taking them—then she was certainly about to find out.

Piper told herself to stop. Instead, she kept walking—and she didn't falter for even a step. As if she'd been waiting for the moment her entire life.

Aching for this moment.

Right up to the moment when her heel snapped off the high heels she'd never quite got used to wearing, and would have sent her tumbling to the ground, if not for Linc catching her fall.

'I can't walk like this,' she muttered, not sure if it was embarrassment or frustration that she felt the most potently.

'Hold on,' he gritted, and placed her arms around his neck.

And then, before she could ask him what he was doing, he simply lifted her up as if she were as light as air to him. Any thoughts began to seep out of Piper's brain. All she could think about were his strong arms around her; and how solid, how unyielding, his chest felt against her body.

She ran her tongue around her suddenly parched mouth. Not that it made it any easier to speak in anything approaching her usual voice.

'What…do you think you're doing, Patch?'

As if using his nickname could shift this…*thing* vibrating inside her. As if it could remind her of that nagging voice that was now shoved to the back of her brain; and she couldn't quite hear what it was trying to say, even if she'd wanted to.

But all Linc did was offer a wordless smile— a dark, utterly masculine curve of his mouth— before striding across the room to shoulder open a discreet door that she hadn't even noticed existed.

Craning her neck, she peered down the long, quiet, spine of a corridor that was presumably the servants' route through the house. A way of getting around quicky and easily, without cluttering up the main hallways where the gentry would be.

As if proving her theory, Linc made straight for a narrow, spiral staircase, and there was something so thrilling about the focussed look in his gaze, and the effortless way that he was carrying her, that made her feel ridiculously feminine, and…obedient. And made her forget everything else.

And then, finally, they were back in their suite. Alone.

'Should we really be doing this, Linc?' she whispered.

'I want you,' he answered simply, his deep voice grazing deliciously over her as surely as if he'd used his teeth.

'Here?' she whispered. 'Now?'

'Here,' he growled in confirmation. 'Now.'

He unzipped her dress, the deliciously naughty sound of it filling the room. Then he slid her dress off her shoulders, stripping her. But it wasn't a race—oh, no—instead, Linc worked painstakingly carefully, pressing his mouth to taste each newly exposed part of her, lavishing attention on every single inch of her bare skin, and taking his time as if he could have feasted on her for ever.

It was a dizzying, glorious notion.

Piper gave herself up to the feel of his lips, his mouth, his tongue inching his way over her flesh as though they had a lifetime to indulge. Maybe two. He tasted her and teased her, tracing exquisite patterns down the long line of her neck, and over her shoulders, his fingers brushing up and down her arms, and she gave herself up to the dazzling sensations that were ricocheting around her body.

It was as though he intended to learn every bit of her, from her forehead to her chin, and from her jawline to her collarbone, he kissed her. Soft, hot brushes of his mouth that sent shock waves through her every single time. And if a century or more had passed them by, then Piper wouldn't have cared.

Then, at last, he turned her round. Inch by stirring inch whilst he slid her dress lower to expose her spine, and then spent perhaps another entire century pressing his lips to the skin there and lavishing attention as he made his way carefully down.

And all she could do was obey. And feel. And marvel.

Never in her life had she known that the mere act of undressing a person could be so electrifying. So indulgent. This bit was the means to the end. The rushed bit of foreplay that was over and gone before she could even blink.

But Linc made it an art form all on its own.

A teasing, thrilling, stirring show that stoked the already smouldering fires in her higher and higher. She wanted more. So much more, and so very badly, that as his mouth moved lower, her dress pooling at her feet as he turned her back around to face him, she feared she would start shaking with desire.

She was sure that she shook with need, and still Linc took his sweet time, giving the removal of those lacy scraps of underwear as much painstaking time as when he removed her gown.

And then, when she was finally naked in front of him, he lifted one leg, kissing down her thigh, and her shin, before moving his mouth to inside and making his way back up again. Closer and closer to where she was aching, *actually aching*, for him the most. But he skimmed past it and when Piper heard a muffled sound, it took her a moment to realise that it was her own voice.

As he repeated the exploration down her other leg, all she could do was grip her shoulders with her hands and wait, just wait, for him to make his way back up again. And if she'd stopped breathing somewhere along the line, then there was nothing she could do about that.

Then, at long last, he was there. His lips inching their way up the inside of her thigh. Higher. Higher. And suddenly, his mouth was right there, at the apex of her legs, where she was molten, and sweet, and yearning for him—and finally, he slid her leg over his shoulder, pressed his mouth to her core, and he feasted on her.

Piper wasn't sure how she stayed standing. She heard her own rasped breathing as his wicked tongue did things to her that she had only ever dreamed of. And not even in such incredible detail. He was toying with her body in ways she hadn't even known were possible, and she wasn't sure she would ever be the same again.

She didn't want to be.

She only wanted this. *Him.* And if everything else simply faded out of existence, then Piper couldn't have cared less. And still, he played with her, driving her on faster, harder.

Her raspy breaths turned to gasps, and cries. At some point she must have slid her fingers into his hair as if that could somehow offer her purchase, as he finally toppled her, high and fast, into blissful oblivion.

By the time Piper came back to herself, she realised he must have carried her across the room to the bed, and he'd laid her down, and rid himself of his suit.

She watched, almost hungrily, as he moved to the end of the bed. Naked, and proud, and every bit as magnificent as she'd pretended not to imagine him to be.

'Are you ready for this, Piper?' he gritted out, and it occurred to her that he was only just managing to control himself.

The realisation was a liberating one. Pushing herself up onto her elbows, Piper reached out with one arm and hooked him around the neck to pull him down onto the bed.

He was all hers, if only for this one night; she would never get this chance again.

She might as well make the most of it.

CHAPTER THIRTEEN

'Come back to bed.'

Piper jumped guiltily as Linc's hoarse voice floated through the dark. Still, she didn't move, keeping her eyes trained on the blackness of the gardens beyond the window, and her arms wrapped tightly around her body.

As if she could somehow ward off the cold guilt that crept through her.

'That should never have happened,' she muttered quietly.

There was no need to say anything more than that; they both knew she was referring to the fact they'd just slept together. Well, not so much *slept*… But the truth was that she wouldn't have changed it even if she could have gone back in time. Just to have that one, perfect night with Linc had to be worth it.

So what did that say about her moral fibre?

Piper heard the rustle of bedsheets, and the soft padding of his feet as Linc crossed the room to her. She still didn't turn around, but then she didn't try to stop him either.

'What's going on, Piper?'

She shook her head, searching for the right words.

'I just…' She steeled her shoulders, hating herself more than ever. 'I haven't been honest with you. I never thought things would get this far. I should never have let them get this far.'

'So be honest with me now.'

His easy tone took her breath away. As if he thought that whatever it was, they could get through it together.

More likely she was just projecting.

'I lied to you about my family,' she blurted out, hating herself. 'That is, not lied exactly; more, omitted.'

He didn't answer, but his hands moved to her shoulders. As though *he* wanted to soothe *her*. It was an odd notion, though not an unpleasant one, though she was too accustomed to being the one taking care of others to really appreciate someone else taking care of her.

Or give herself up to the temptation.

Carefully, she moved to the side and away, trying to put a little distance between them. All the same, when he didn't close the gap again, she felt strangely…bereft.

'I'm all wrong for you. We come from different worlds.'

Linc shook his head.

'No, we come from the same world, you and I. First the military world, now the Helimed world.'

'You're the son of a duke, Lincoln,' she burst out.

'Accepting that I'm his son and not just my

mother's unwanted kid, then I'm the second son of a duke, which, to all intents and purposes, means very little. I'll never become the duke—that's my brother's role, not that he wants it either. But he has no choice.'

'You're still a lord. And I'm...'

'You're what? A bright, intelligent woman? A skilled pilot? A beautiful human being, inside and out? Take your pick, Piper; just don't start any nonsense about not being good enough for a lord because, trust me, titles don't mean anything.'

'Nonetheless...' Her teeth were worrying at her lower lip so hard it was beginning to chafe. She forced herself to stop. 'I'm not the person you think I am.'

'That doesn't even make sense, Legs. You're overthinking things.'

'No, I'm not.' She shook her head, trying to stop the shaking from overtaking her entire body.

She had to do this, no matter how unpalatable it was.

'I once told you that my father died.'

'You did,' he agreed after a moment's thought.

'What I didn't mention was that my mother was accused of killing him,' she confessed heavily, resenting every word that was coming out of her mouth.

'Say that again?'

She found the barely concealed horror in his tone disheartening. Or was she just imagining it would be there? And then, as suddenly as her moment of boldness had come, it disappeared again. Without warning, she swayed, and stumbled, and just as she felt herself about to crash to the floor she felt two strong arms catch her and carry her to the wingback chairs that overlooked the expansive gardens.

It was surely the height of irony that staring at them through the bars of the lead-paned windows was as though she were staring at them from behind the bars of her very own prison.

Piper gritted her teeth and forced herself to speak.

'It wasn't true, of course,' she managed. 'It didn't take much for the police to realise that my mother would never have hurt my father. Though I wouldn't have blamed her if she had.'

'You're going too fast, Piper,' Linc rumbled. 'Back up a few steps and tell me from the start.'

But she couldn't. Her mind was spiralling and her mouth seemed hell-bent on blurting out whichever details popped into her head first.

'The point is that I should never have come here and pretended to be your fiancée,' she rushed on. 'And when we were on the beach and you told me about your mother and how bad a scandal would be for your family, I should have told you then. At the very least, I should never have slept with you. That was wrong and I'm…sorry.'

Or at least, she really ought to be. She shouldn't

be neatly wrapping up what had just happened between them into some perfect memory she could open up in the future and replay. Relive.

'Piper, stop. Breathe.'

Linc's voice cut into her thoughts and she realised she'd been speaking faster and faster, as though putting it all out there as fast as possible could get this whole ordeal over with sooner.

As if Linc wouldn't have a mine of questions.

'Sorry,' she muttered, struggling to catch her breath.

'Just take your time, Piper. Start from the beginning and explain it to me. All of it.'

And it was the quiet empathy in his tone that struck her more than anything. Very much as though he cared.

Ridiculous notion.

'I don't know where to start,' she admitted, after a moment, splaying out her hands helplessly. 'I'm sorry, I just...'

'It's fine, let me help,' he soothed, and she wondered how he could be so calm after what she'd just said. 'You once told me that you had a good childhood. You said that there was a lot of love, if not a lot of money.'

'I did,' Piper managed miserably, though the words felt strange in her mouth. Thick, and heavy, and gloopy. 'And that was true, for the most part.'

She lifted her shoulders helplessly. It wasn't that she didn't *want* to tell him the truth—for the first time in her life she'd found someone she actually felt she could explain it to—it was more that she had no idea *how* she was supposed to tell him. How she was even to begin to explain. Words swirled around her head, but she couldn't seem to make any of them come out of her mouth.

'I actually have a sister as well as my brother. She's three years older than me but we don't get on any longer. She and I grew up with my parents in a small terraced house on a housing estate. My sister was the pretty one, the bold one, the funny one, she charmed everyone she met within moments, and I adored her. Everyone adored her. But my father was the one she loved most—a daddy's girl from the start—whilst I was closer to my mother. I was quieter, more reserved, like my mother. He loved us all, of course, but not the same way.'

She paused, trying to slow her racing pulse and order her thoughts. All the while, Linc knelt quietly opposite her, his hands at her elbows as though he wasn't appalled by the very sight of her. She wondered what must be going through his head.

'I was fifteen when my father was in an industrial accident. He lost part of his right hand and his job. He'd been a manual labourer all his life, and without his hand, he'd now lost his job, and couldn't provide for his family.'

'What about compensation?' Linc asked. 'If it

was an industrial accident, surely he should have got a payout?'

'The company couldn't afford it and so they declared bankruptcy. There was nothing my father could do. He'd always been a proud man, but then he found himself thirty-eight, unable to work.'

'What happened, Piper?'

She took a breath, beating back the memories that she'd pushed away for so long. Carefully locked behind a thick door in her mind, where they couldn't get to her. Couldn't hurt her.

'We didn't have much money. My brother hadn't even been born but my mum worked a waitressing job already, and she got a second one cleaning an office block in the evenings. I got a job in a local corner shop.'

'And your sister?'

'She'd moved out when she was eighteen, just before Dad's accident. She'd met a boy, fallen for him, got pregnant, and got married. He'd landed a job at an oil refinery across the country, so they'd moved away.'

'So she couldn't help,' Linc noted.

'No, but I don't think anyone could have given that he didn't tell them. He didn't even tell my mum. He pretended that he'd got a job but borrowed money from a loan shark,' she bit out. 'I can only imagine that he thought it would tide him over until he really did find something. But then the next month came and he borrowed more.

And the month after that. I think that was when he started drinking.'

'Your father became an alcoholic,' Linc guessed.

Piper jerked her head stiffly, hating that she had to confirm it.

'He'd never really been a drinker, but I guess he found it numbed his brain and helped him to forget his situation. But he was a mean drunk.'

'By *mean*, I'm guessing you mean violent? Abusive?' Linc gritted his teeth, as though he was angry on her behalf.

It was…unexpectedly endearing, Piper thought dimly.

'Not to my brother or to me, but to Mum.' She didn't care to go into too much detail, but that didn't mean the memories weren't there. The screams, the sight of him, the fear for her mother. 'It didn't help that she just kept making excuses for him, and practically killed herself doing everything he demanded to keep him happy. She fell pregnant at the age of forty-two with my younger brother.'

Piper didn't elaborate, the look on Linc's face—reflected in the moonlight—assured her that he understood.

'I tried to get her to leave so many times, but she just kept saying she'd taken a marriage vow with him. *In sickness and in health*, and that he was sick. Even when he broke her arm, she just said that he was sick and that it was her role to take care of him.'

'I'm so sorry, Legs,' Linc growled. And she found herself smiling—albeit weakly—at the nickname, just as she suspected he'd intended that she would.

It was a moment of levity that she'd needed. Sucking in a deep breath, she pressed on.

'I think it would have been different if he'd ever tried to hurt me, or my brother,' Piper mused. 'I think she'd have left straight away. I'd like to think so, anyway.'

'So he never touched either of you kids?'

'Never.' Not that it lessened what he'd done to her mother. 'One night when he had put her in the hospital for the umpteenth time, I decided enough was enough. The hospital recognised the type of injury and they sent in a social worker as they always did, but this time I refused to cover for him. I told them what was happening, then I contacted our sister and I told her too.'

There was no way that Piper could keep the sorrow out of her voice, nor the tinge of anger, no matter how she tried.

'She said I was lying. That I was mistaken. She argued that if Dad was going through a hard time, then it was because he'd been through such a traumatic accident, and Mum ought to take better care of him and have more empathy.'

'She can't have really believed that.'

'I don't know.' Piper shrugged. 'Maybe she did. She never personally saw that side of him. To her, he was a quiet, gentle man who wouldn't even kill a spider in the bathtub. He used to take them outside and release them into the garden.'

'Events can change people, Piper. Not always for the better.'

Piper pulled her lips into a tight line, as though that could somehow ward off the sadness of the memories.

'I know that. I suppose my sister simply didn't want to see the truth. So she said it wasn't possible.'

'Your mum didn't collaborate your story to the social worker either,' he growled. 'Did she?'

Slowly, Piper moved her head from side to side.

'No, she refused to back me up. She claimed she'd been in the house alone, vacuuming the stairs, when she'd tangled her feet up in the hose and fallen. We all knew she was lying, but without her speaking out against my father, no one could do anything about it.'

'So you all went back home together.'

'We did. Mum didn't talk to me, except to say that she would never forgive me. She could barely even look at me. But, for a while, it was okay. I think maybe me telling the truth had scared him. Even if no one could act without my mum admitting it, he knew I wasn't going to be complicit.'

'It didn't last though, did it?' Linc demanded. 'It couldn't. He wasn't going to change.'

And the bleak expression on his face reminded her that, in her own way, Linc's mother had been just as cruel and abusive. It was just that hers was mental abuse rather than physical.

They each had their demons, her and Linc. How had it taken all these years to realise that?

'Eventually, he couldn't keep it up and the cycle started again. I was seventeen and desperate to join the army as soon as I could, but I was afraid what he'd do if I left him alone with her. Or with my baby brother. I tried to get her to leave again. To say something. To do something, but she wouldn't. Then, one night, when I was out at work, he came in steaming drunk as usual, but he'd run out of money.'

She squeezed her eyes shut as the memory slammed into her, and a wave of nausea threatened to overwhelm her.

'It was bad, wasn't it?' Linc growled, though his hand didn't stop caressing hers.

It was an unexpected comfort.

'The worst it had ever been,' she admitted, swallowing hard. 'I…'

'You don't need to go into details if you aren't ready.'

She nodded, grateful.

'I threw the money I'd earned that day at him, and grabbed the baby, then I got Mum out of there.

I didn't really have a plan, I just thought we could go to a halfway house or a shelter, or something. We were just leaving the front gate when we heard the smash. I don't know what possessed me to go back inside. I think it was the eeriness of the silence that followed. Just…nothing. But when I peered around the doorway, I saw he'd fallen into the coffee table and as it had smashed, a shard of glass penetrated his femoral, a little like that motocross kid on the first shout we did, really.'

'He bled out?'

'We tried to stem it. We got some tea towels and tried to apply pressure, but neither of us really knew what to do back then. By the time the police and ambulance arrived, he was dead.'

'There was nothing more you could have done with that kind of injury,' Linc managed gruffly.

Piper didn't answer. Logically, she knew that was true, but it didn't always help.

'How could they possibly have accused your mother of killing him, though?' Linc frowned.

And perhaps this was the worst of it all. Piper inhaled deeply.

'They didn't. My sister did.'

'Your sister wasn't even there.' Linc sounded infuriated.

'No, but she couldn't accept it had been an accident. She insisted we must have done something to him. Even when two different neighbours concurred that they'd heard him still shouting in the house when we were on the driveway, and then the crash, she refused to let it go. She has always blamed my mother for living when my father died, and she has never accepted the truth.'

She'd even tried to win custody of their baby brother, claiming that their mother was unfit for the role. But Linc didn't need to know that additional sordid secret. He already had enough gory truths to disgust him about her family.

'I'm only telling you all of this so that you understand why I should go. Why I have to leave now. Before any of this comes to bite your family.' She shifted on her chair, but Linc didn't move. He caged her, without even touching it.

Or perhaps it was simply that a traitorous part of her wanted to pretend that he was stopping her from going.

Oh, she never should have come.

'I'm so sorry that happened to you.' Linc lifted his hand to her chin, cupping it.

Piper twisted her mouth awkwardly and stayed silent.

What else was there to say?

He dropped his hand. 'I promise you, as soon as we get back to Heathston, I'll help you find a place for your mother and your brother to move to, so they can be closer to you now.'

'No,' she bit out. Loudly. 'I don't need your help. I can look after my family myself. If this job in West Nessleton comes through, we'll be fine.'

'You don't need to leave,' he argued softly.

And dammit if all she wanted to do was believe him.

She stamped the urge out viciously.

'Of course I do. I'm a landmine in your family just waiting for someone to detonate it. And you said it yourself today. The last thing your family needs right now is more scandals to make the board topple Raf. I'll head back to Heathston tonight and I'll find somewhere else to live. You need to stay here and come up with some plausible reason as to why I can't come to the wedding next week.'

'Legs...'

She shook her head, refusing to listen.

'The sooner we go our own ways, the better. And I think your plan of moving back here to be closer to your family and set up a new Helimed for the region is a great idea.'

'Piper.' His voice was still quiet, but this time it was firmer.

Enough to silence her.

But she still didn't look at him until he hooked his fingers under her chin and lifted it up.

'I don't care about your past,' he told her. 'I certainly don't care about dragging up a horrid past that no one should ever have had to go through, least of all a mother you've always said was kind, and generous, and good.'

'That's admirable.' She tried to pull her face

away but found she couldn't. For all her attempt to resist him, she couldn't bring herself to break that contact. 'But you know what they say: mud sticks, and all that.'

'Then turn it into a cleansing mud treatment.' Linc shrugged. 'My sister claims they're all the rage.'

'It isn't a joke.' Piper blinked at him.

'Perhaps not. But nor is it the end of the world, the way you're telling yourself it is. I want you. I like you. And you like me, too.'

'But you said it yourself, your family have endured enough scandal with everything your mother did. If they should dig up my past, then everything we did here to try to help your brother will have been for nothing.'

'I highly doubt anyone will delve into your past, Piper.'

'They might.' She jutted out her chin. 'You can't risk it. You said it yourself, there are people looking to discredit you just so they can get your shares.'

'And Raf and I have talked and come up with a way to deal with them. Me being here with you has gone a long way to helping that. So come back to bed, Piper. No one will care about me by tomorrow, or who I date. And no one will care about your secret. You're safe with me.'

And it was tempting, oh, so tempting, to just obey. To put the ugliness behind her and simply be with Linc. Be herself. Because it was true, she did feel safe with Linc.

She just wasn't sure he was entirely safe with her.

'I can't...' she forced herself to say.

He slid his hands down her legs, straightening them out so that he could help her to her feet. As though he could help her to move on.

God, she should have told him the whole truth. Everything. Even that last part about her sister. If she ever discovered that Piper was dating someone like Linc—that she was happy—Piper didn't think there was anything her sister wouldn't stoop to in order to take away that happiness.

It had never before occurred to her that her sister was acting out of her own sense of guilt.

'Linc, wait.' She faltered, hating this bit more than anything. 'There's something else.'

'I don't want to hear more.' He stopped her with his mouth. His tongue dipping so enticingly into her mouth. 'It's your past, Piper. Let it stay there.'

'But...'

'Just enjoy this for what it is,' he growled, dropping kisses from her mouth to move lower, to that sweet spot just on the column of her neck. 'For however long it lasts.'

And later she would think it was that last remark that convinced her to stay quiet. Even though a part of her wanted to tell him the truth, he was making her brain go fuzzy. Her thoughts dissolving into sheer sensation.

And, as he said, there was no need for everything to be laid out there. They were having fun for now. It wasn't as if this relationship could ever really go anywhere.

She ought to be grateful to him for reminding her of that fact.

And even though she wasn't convinced Linc was entirely thinking things through—even though she knew the moral thing to do would be to walk away, the way she should have done two weeks ago—she let him lower his mouth down to hers.

She let him, and she surrendered to him.

Because she might have wanted to listen to her head…but right now, her traitorous heart was the one in control.

CHAPTER FOURTEEN

'Anyone see anything?'

Piper brought the heli around as all four members of the team scanned the ground below them for signs of their new patient. Not helped by the hazy mist that was beginning to roll in over these mountains.

'Nothing this side,' Probie answered over the headset.

'Nor this side,' added Tom.

'Can you take us back up a little higher?' Linc's voice rumbled. 'I might have something, though it's a little further south-east than the caller said it was.'

Piper duly took the bird up, her eyes still expertly scanning the ground even as she considered how well they were working together these days. Better than ever, she might even say.

It had been almost a week since she and Linc had returned from Oakenfeld Hall, and neither of them had raised the subject of her family since then. Instead, they'd spent their days pretending to their colleagues they were still nothing more than friends, but their nights exploring every inch of each other.

Piper thought that Linc had probably learned

every line and every contour of her body, first with his wicked hands, then with his even more wicked tongue. Not that it made each night any less of a revelation. Another journey of exploration. And she couldn't imagine ever tiring of such adventures.

Still, she didn't know what it meant. Linc hadn't mentioned his idea of him returning to his home since the evening of the wedding rehearsal. Had he changed his mind since things between the two of them had shifted? Or was he simply waiting for whatever this...*thing* was between them to peter out?

Sometimes Piper thought she didn't want to know. Other times, she thought the uncertainty could drive her insane.

Or perhaps that was just the guilt, eating away at her no matter how many times she tried to stuff it back down. Ultimately, it would ruin everything, she knew that. And still, she couldn't bring herself to do anything about it. As if gorging on her time with Linc could somehow save her from when it all fell apart.

And it would.

'See better now?' Piper asked, having taken the heli up to a better height. Not so high that it made things too small to see, but enough to give them a clearer, longer view. 'The caller said she wasn't familiar with this range. If her walking partner fell the opposite side to the one she thought, she could have given us the wrong info.'

Linc leaned forward, peering closer.

'Yeah, pretty sure I saw a flash of blue over there, two o'clock position.'

Piper followed his direction. It certainly looked as if someone might be down there, behind a mid-sized outcrop. Probably hoping to take shelter from the downdraught of the rotors, without re-alising they didn't actually know where their casualty was.

'Can you take a fly around?' Linc asked. 'Or is it too close to that rock face?'

'I wouldn't like to go all the way around. There might be loose rocks. But I can certainly bring her round a little more.'

'It isn't the best place to land down here,' noted Linc. 'If that blue *is* them, we might have a bit of a trek in.'

She'd been thinking the same thing. Down at this level the ground was too uneven for the heli. The only flat area she'd seen was too close to the sharp mountain face, which meant there was a good chance she would have to take the heli back to the top and let the crew either make their way down the long, winding path, or abseil.

Usually, it was mountain rescue heli that op-erated in these parts, but they'd been called to a shout just out to sea with a man overboard.

'Let's see if we've got the right people.' Piper

grimaced as she manoeuvred her heli into a better position. 'Anyone got a clear view?'

'Yeah, that's our guy,' Linc confirmed after a moment as he called it in, whilst Piper backed the heli away and looked more earnestly for somewhere to land. 'Hotel zero seven, this is Helimed hotel one-niner, over, ready with an update, over.'

'Go ahead, hotel one-niner.'

'We've located the casualty but the ground is too rocky to land close by. Confirm a land mountain rescue crew is on their way, over?'

'Yeah, that's confirmed, Helimed hotel one-niner, they should be with you within the next fifteen to twenty minutes, over.'

Piper waited for Linc to conclude the call.

'I want to head down this valley a way,' she told him. 'I think I saw a flatter area on the way in, which wouldn't make it any faster for you guys to get to the casualty, but it would make evacuation a lot easier if you don't have to get them back up the mountainside.'

'How long?'

'Not long,' she assured him. 'I know time is of the essence.'

Turning the nose in the direction she wanted, Piper flew as efficiently as she could. Sure enough, the flat area she hoped for came into view quickly.

'Here okay?'

'Yeah, great. Well spotted,' Linc agreed. 'Take us down.'

She didn't need to be told twice. Quickly, skilfully, she turned her heli until it was on the granite plateau.

'You make that look a damned sight easier than it is,' Linc complimented as he opened the door and bundled out with his bag.

And Piper tried not to flush like the kind of giggly schoolgirl she couldn't remember ever having been, as he cast her a wink that only the two of them shared.

She might have known it couldn't last.

It was late by the time Linc arrived home—and wasn't the truth of it now that it really did feel like a home, not just a penthouse, since Piper had moved in?

But his anticipation was short-lived when he walked through the door to see Piper looking ashen, and Sara glaring at her as if she were something not even the stable cat would deign to drag in. He had a feeling it was only Raf's presence that was keeping things from degenerating further.

And it should have concerned him—that dark sensation that pierced straight through his body at the thought that someone had hurt Piper.

He wanted to wring them out for their audacity, no matter who they were. Even his sister.

'Care to tell me what's going on?'

His voice might be silky smooth, but surely

no one could have missed the warning note that threaded through it. Not even bull-headed Sara.

'This…woman—' Sara spat the word out as though it were poison in her mouth '—could destroy our family.'

'I suggest you're a little more careful concerning what you say about my guests in my home,' he managed, the warning note even clearer.

But it seemed that his sister was even more obstinate than he'd anticipated.

'You should steer clear, Linc. She isn't who she pretends to be. Her name isn't even Piper Green. Did you know that?'

'I did not,' Linc acknowledged as casually as he could whilst he turned to Piper. 'You took your mother's name after his death, presumably?'

She blinked at him, and he realised she'd been expecting accusations.

'I did.' Her voice cracked.

He took a step closer as if to lend her his support, but she refused to even look his way. It didn't matter, he could read the shame in every line of her body, and he balled his fists into his pockets as though that could somehow contain his anger.

He loathed the sight of the scarlet stain that stole cruelly over Piper's cheeks. He knew how it felt. He'd felt the same way when his mother had announced with such delight that he wasn't even his father's biological son.

'So that explains the name,' he turned to his

sister coolly. 'And I'm also aware of her father's death. After all, that was going to be your next question, was it not?'

'What do you mean, you're aware?' Sara's voice pitched higher.

'I already know what you're going to say,' Linc clipped out. 'Piper told me herself. The question is why were you nosing in her private business?'

'Because unlike you, I believe it's prudent to know about the people trying to insinuate themselves into our lives. And if you know, then you should have told me. And Raf.'

'I wholly disagree.' He forced a casual note into his voice, knowing it would lodge itself under his sister's skin with far more effect than raising his voice to her. 'I know Piper's past because she chose to tell me herself. And I didn't choose to share it because I determined that it wasn't our business. Though I'm surprised at you, Raf.'

'No.' Raf shook his head, taking a step away. 'Not me. I just wanted to be sure you knew about it. If you do, and you're happy you know the truth, then I am too. I trust you.'

Any remaining words Linc had for his brother died on his lips as Raf turned to Piper and offered her an equally dignified apology before turning to Sara.

'We should leave now. Linc knows, we have our answer. Piper, you have my apologies.'

'Well, you don't have mine,' Sara snapped. 'I'm

not going anywhere until Lincoln realises exactly how this…phony has played him.'

'Then you're doing it alone,' Raf growled, taking his leave with only a final nod of his head to Piper, causing Sara to turn back on her.

'I trusted you. I told you that I was *happy* you were in my brother's life.'

Linc blinked in surprise.

'Did she really say that to you?'

And, finally, his beautiful Piper lifted her head and met his sister's glower head-on.

'You told me that maybe you had misjudged me, and that perhaps I wasn't such a poor decision for your brother, after all,' Piper managed, every word like glass in her mouth. 'And I didn't have the decency to tell you that you hadn't misjudged me at all. I should never have gone to your wedding rehearsal, and for that, I truly am sorry.'

'You don't owe anyone an apology,' Linc growled, his ribcage tightening at the misery in her expressive eyes.

'I do. I told you my past could damage your family, and I was right.'

'It hasn't damaged anything. What was it you told me, Piper—that I didn't carry anyone else's sins but my own?'

'It isn't the same thing,' Sara blasted out furiously. 'She helped to kill her own father.'

Beside him, he heard Piper's sharp intake of breath, her anguished gurgle. He wasn't sure how he manged not to bodily eject his sister from his penthouse, there and then.

They both knew there was only one person Sara could have got that information from. But surely even his sister wouldn't have gone that far.

'You have no idea what you're talking about,' he ground out coldly.

'I know she and her excuse of a mother covered up what they did.'

'Since when do we blame victims of abuse, Sara?' he managed icily. 'And, for the record, Piper wasn't even there when it all happened.'

And right now, he could only imagine what had to be going through Piper's head.

His Piper.

The realisation walloped through him, leaving him almost light-headed. He needed to talk to Piper alone. Sara needed to go. Striding across the room, he flung open his penthouse door.

He was throwing his sister out twice in as many weeks, but there was nothing else for it.

'I also suggest you follow Raf's lead, and leave.'

It was the most controlled thing he could think of to say. Moving back across the room, he put his arms around Piper, his entire body feeling it when she stiffened against his touch, as though she was barely stopping herself from ducking away.

And all he wanted was his sister gone so that he could make Piper talk to him. Make him understand that his sister had no right to do what she was doing.

'You're choosing her over us?' Sara pulled a disgusted face. 'You can't do that.'

'Then I suggest you don't make me,' he warned her. 'Get out, before either of us say or do something which we might regret.'

'You can't do this, Linc, I won't let you.'

'Leave. Now.'

She opened her mouth as though ready to respond, before appearing to think better of it. And then, at length, she snatched up her bag and stormed to the door.

'You'll regret choosing her over family.'

'I think not.'

'I don't want her at my wedding.'

'That is regrettable, but it's your wedding. But know that if Piper isn't welcome, then neither am I.'

'Of course you are. You have to be there, you're my brother.'

'If Piper isn't welcome, then neither am I,' he repeated. 'Your choice.'

And he waited, his chest pounding, as his sister finally got the message and left, leaving him and Piper alone.

'You shouldn't have done that,' Piper managed as aftershock wave after aftershock wave slammed through her.

It twisted her tongue, preventing her from answering. She wasn't even sure she could still breathe.

'I had to,' Linc bit out after what felt like an age. 'You were letting her talk to you as if she had a right to say those things.'

'I can't stop her.' Piper pressed her hand to her forehead as if trying to stave off a headache.

Hardly surprising.

'You could have told her the truth. Everything you told me.'

'You aren't serious?' Piper breathed incredulously. 'I told you because I trust you, Linc. I don't want to talk to Sara. It's humiliating enough without having to tell everyone.'

'Sara should never have spoken to you that way, but you could have told her what really happened. Not let your sister keep spreading lies about you and your mother, going unchecked every time.'

Did he know how much he was asking of her? He couldn't possibly. And what did it matter, anyway? What had just happened had been avoidable, if only she'd stayed away from Linc the way that every fibre of her had screamed to do from the start.

Even before he'd told her how far from scandal his family needed to be. Even before he'd told her about his fame-hungry mother.

A bomb like this had always been inevitable, the fallout predictable. And still she'd gone ahead and let herself be with him.

She'd brought it on herself. And she told him as much.

'You did not bring anything on yourself,' Linc declared instantly. 'If anything, my sister brought it on herself. But you should have trusted me to have your back.'

'Why, Linc? Why should I ever have trusted you?'

He stared at her as though she had two heads.

'We're supposed to be a couple.'

Piper snorted derisively, if shakily.

'Fake couple, Linc,' she managed—giving the impression that the words tasted acrid in her mouth. 'There's nothing real about what's between us.'

'I disagree.'

So simple. So certain. It caught her off guard, and for a moment she only stared at him.

Then she offered the faintest shake of her head.

'You're confusing love, and lust, and yearning, I fear,' she managed, with a coldness of her own.

And if he didn't know her as well as he did then he wouldn't have realised that her heart was being ripped out, just as his was.

'Whatever has been between us was sexual attraction, Linc. That was *all* it was. Sex. There was nothing real—nothing substantial. We don't even really know each other.'

'I think we both know that's a lie.' His tone changed.

And as easily as that, all the heat slid out of the situation. Piper stared at him miserably.

'Maybe it was,' she admitted, so quietly that he almost missed it. 'Maybe we did have a chance at something more than just *pretend*. But that's gone now. This was meant to be Sara's wedding week, from her rehearsal last weekend to her wedding this weekend. Now it will be tainted with my squalid past for ever.'

'Trust me.' Linc moved towards her. 'There's nothing my sister will relish more than a meaty story to make her wedding more memorable than any of her friends'.'

'You're wrong.' Piper shook her head. 'We were meant to be a couple to make things go more smoothly, now it will only cause more gossip and upset. If the board members use this to help their coup, do you really think either Sara or Raf will ever relish such a *meaty story*?'

And he hated that she had a point.

'I'll deal with it,' he promised her grimly. 'I think it's clear to her that if you aren't welcome, then neither am I.'

'So you're issuing ultimatums?' Piper challenged sadly. 'That's how you want to handle the wedding of your only sister? By backing her into a corner?'

A dull bellow started in his chest. Was that how it would look to his sister?

'I'm not backing her into any corner.'

'We both know that isn't how Sara will see it.' Piper shook her head. 'And for what it's worth, I think I'd feel the same, in her position.'

The bellowing got louder.

Piper was right, he couldn't force Sara to accept Piper at her wedding. But if he attended alone, then he might as well be giving Sara licence to investigate anyone he ever chose to date.

Can there be anyone else after Piper?

He stuffed the thought away quickly.

But still, she deserved better than this. Better than accusations that neither she nor her mother—both victims in different ways—would ever deserve. And Piper was right, now wasn't the time to punish his sister for trying to look out for him in her own, slightly twisted way. But given the way their mother had always treated her—jealous of her daughter's youth, and acuity, and looks—was it any wonder that Sara had never known quite how to communicate with other women?

Still, right now, his main concern was Piper. If he wanted his family to accept her at all—though if it came down to a choice between the two of them, he knew now that there would only ever be one winner—then he needed to wait until after Sara's honeymoon.

He would attend the wedding alone, avoiding a scene, because it was what Piper wanted. And because he had long since known how to pick his battles.

'This isn't about anyone else,' he ground out. 'This is about you, and it's about me.'

'We both know things aren't that simple,' Piper denied, as the resignation in her tone made his very soul ache.

'Nonetheless, I'll go to the wedding,' he confirmed after a moment, watching the relief chase across Piper's face. 'But only because I won't allow your name to ever become the reason for any distance between my siblings and me.'

'Linc…'

'However, this isn't the end of our conversation, Piper.' He gently lifted her chin so that she could see the promise in his eyes. 'We'll talk when I get back.'

'Yes,' she whispered.

And later, much later, he would wonder if she'd really meant it, or if he'd abjectly failed to read the lie behind that one, simple word that had fallen so easily from her lips.

CHAPTER FIFTEEN

'LET'S GET TO our patient.' Linc leapt out of the heli as soon as Albert landed at the new shout.

Without waiting for a response, he raced across the field and vaulted the drystone wall at the end, and into the residential street, following the direction pointed out by various bystanders.

It had been just over two weeks since his sister's wedding. Over two weeks since he'd returned home to find that his penthouse was empty and Piper had left. The place hadn't felt like home ever since.

Even now, he didn't know whether she'd gone the moment he'd walked out of the door, or whether she'd left the next day, when the story her sister had sold to the press about the undeserving Piper bagging herself a lord had hit the gutter press.

But the question that really ate away at him was why she hadn't taken any of his calls, even when she'd realised that the story hadn't gone anywhere—especially when the few desperate journalists who *had* tried to follow up on the piece had realised that both he and Piper had served together in theatres of war.

The potentially 'juicy scandal' had faded into

obscurity as quickly as it had appeared. No one
had cared, least of all his brother, or the Oakenfeld board. In fact, if anything, it had made the old
cronies review him in a different light—a military hero who could be an asset to Oakenfeld Industries. Linc couldn't say he cared for the image
change but if it meant Piper would be free of any
hounding—and Raf would be given a boost—then
he was prepared not to argue.

But what had really come home to Linc was
that he wouldn't have cared what anyone had said.
The only person he'd realised he truly cared about
was Piper. She had gazed into that dark void in
his soul, but instead of fearing it she had flooded
it with light, with warmth, with *Piper*. Without
her, he wasn't even sure he felt whole.

So tonight, at last, he was determined to find
her in person—no more unanswered phone
calls—and tell her. He'd given Piper long enough
to come around to his way of thinking, to come
back to him on her own. Now it was finally time
to go out and bring her home. It was likely the
only thing that would make him feel he could
breathe again.

Even the return of Albert had only just taken
the edge off his sense of disquiet—the old pilot
slipping back into his role with obvious relief.

Rounding the corner, Linc hurried to where
a paramedic—one of the land crew already on
scene—was signalling to him. He could already

see the patient over her shoulder as the man lay groaning on the ground.

'This is Jez?' Linc surmised.

'Yes,' the paramedic confirmed as she led Linc over. 'Jez is a normally fit and well forty-year-old male. Approximately thirty minutes ago he was on the roof of his home repairing the mortar around the chimney stack when he slipped and fell around ten metres onto the flower bed below.'

'Loss of consciousness?'

'None reported.' The paramedic shook her head. 'He's talked us through events and there doesn't appear to be any loss of memory. He's complaining of mild back pain. He is able to breathe deeply and there is good bilateral air flow. I'm concerned about a laceration to the back of his head, but he isn't complaining of any head pain.'

Linc glanced over to the patient, who was still lying on his side.

'No collar?'

'I didn't want to move him until you got here, in case he had a spinal injury.'

'Okay, thanks.' Linc nodded, indicating to Tom and Probie to approach the patient. 'Hello, Jez, I'm Linc, the air ambulance doctor. Mind if we take a quick look at you?'

He crouched down on the opposite side of the patient to Tom, and the two of them began their assessment.

'Can you tell me what happened, Jez?'

The man talked them through the accident with surprising accuracy and calmness.

'And on a scale of one to ten, Jez, if one is mild, and ten is the worst pain you can imagine, can you tell me what your pain level is?'

'I dunno, Doc,' the man pondered slowly. 'It isn't bad actually. It's more of a dull ache around my back. About one. Not much more.'

Linc and Tom exchanged a glance but didn't speak. Given the height of his fall, and the way the man had landed, if his pain wasn't acute then he was either miraculously lucky, or he'd done some serious damage that was preventing him from feeling the pain.

'I'd like to get him out of this narrow passage-way so that we can examine him more easily,' Linc told the crew. 'Best thing is going to be to get him on a scoop and to a level part of the garden. Tom, can you hold the neck whilst we turn him and then we'll get a collar on as soon as we can?'

The team worked quickly and efficiently, work-ing together to get the patient onto the scoop without causing any further injury to what was potentially a serious neck problem. Soon, they had Jez on the flatter part of the lawn with better access around him, and began a more thorough examination. The most concerning discovery was that the man seemed to have damaged his C-Four and C-Five neck vertebrae, which was impairing his body's ability to transmit the pain.

A false move, and there was a chance their patient could end up being paralysed.

'Okay, Jez.' Linc moved over his patient until the man could see him. 'We're concerned you may have injured your neck, so we're going to keep your head stable with some tape, as well as the collar.'

'Okay, Doc.'

'We're going to get you in the air ambulance now, and get you straight to Heathston Royal Infirmary, okay?'

For the moment, despite the laceration on the back of Jez's head, the man's good cognitive function didn't suggest any major head injury. But without full scans and X-rays at the major trauma unit, Linc couldn't rule out the possibility of a brain bleed.

The sooner they got their patient to hospital, the better.

Piper huddled down in the seat of her car as she watched Linc and Albert in the distance, whilst they pulled the helicopter back in after their shift.

It had been a little over a fortnight since she'd last seen him—as if she didn't know it right down to the days and hours. Possibly the worst time of her life, if she was going to be honest—which was saying something. And every day she'd had a moment of weakness when she'd almost, *almost*, taken his phone calls, or picked up the phone herself.

Somehow she'd resisted. Until now. Until the letter—the job offer—that had arrived in her barracks' post box this morning. Not just any offer, but the offer of a job at Stoneywell air ambulance—with Linc as the critical care doctor, just as he'd once suggested.

Her heart rattled against her ribs with nervous anticipation. She needed to know if he just wanted a pilot, or if he wanted something more from her as well.

Piper shifted again in her seat, and eyed the car clock as Linc dropped the handle to the trailer and headed inside to complete his paperwork whilst the old pilot completed the last of the post-shift checks.

The rest of the crew would be leaving within the next half-hour or so, leaving Linc alone in the base. And then she was determined to go and speak to him—despite her jangling nerves.

Because the truth was that she'd had plenty of time to think these past couple of weeks. Plenty of time to realise that sneaking out of Linc's penthouse the day after his sister's wedding—the day that first venomous piece from her sister had come out—hadn't been her finest hour.

In truth, she felt it had been the biggest mistake of her life, not least because every inch of her had missed that maddening, thrilling, gorgeous man, every second since she'd done it. It had taken her more steel than she'd ever known—even flying her Apaches in war zones—to ignore her phone every time his ringtone had shattered the semblance of peace that she'd pulled around herself.

Only, perhaps he hadn't missed her the same way. Perhaps he'd been calling to detail exactly the damage that her sister's story had done to him. And to his family's name. Little wonder that she was ashamed at herself for lacking the moral fibre to take his calls and find out, and even less surprise that, after a while, he'd stopped calling altogether.

Clearly he must have realised that his life was far less complicated—far less messy—without her in it.

At least, if there was such a thing as a silver lining, the press didn't seem to have published anything more than that one single story. She'd scoured the newspapers every day since yet, to her shock, nothing new seemed to have been written.

And finally, *finally*, Piper had started to try to breathe once again. Enough to regret running from the man who had stood by her even against his own family that last night. But the more time had passed, the more it had felt as if it was too late to change it.

Until now.

Instinctively, Piper's fingers felt for the letter in her pocket. Linc might not have sent it personally but it felt like an olive branch, all the same. A last chance. And what did it say about her feelings for Linc that she had jumped into her car and travelled all the way back to Heathston to speak to him, instead of simply picking up a phone?

Piper started as the door to the base burst open and Probie sauntered out, followed by Hugo. She hunkered down in her seat hoping they wouldn't spot her car, nestled as it was between an old airport minivan and the fence line. But they were too caught up in their own conversations to look her way, and within minutes they were gone.

A short while later, both Tom and then Albert followed.

Which only left Linc.

Her heart lodged somewhere between her chest and her throat, Piper folded her legs out of her car and hurried towards the base door. She was halfway across the tarmac when she spotted him. Lolling on his muscular motorbike and waiting as though he had all the time in the world.

For her.

The others might not have spotted her, but Linc hadn't missed her.

A part of her wanted to turn around and run in the opposite direction. Another part of her wanted to run to him. In the end, she merely hesitated and then walked slowly over, pretending that her entire body didn't notice when he stood up, feet apart and arms folded over a simple black tee that only served to enhance that utterly male body and remind her of the last time she'd explored every inch of it.

But her palms didn't itch—she wouldn't allow them to. She refused to remember just how it had felt, running her hands all over this man's body, again and again, as though she had a thirst that only he could sate.

And she told herself that, for all her apprehension, she hadn't imagined this moment—seeing him again—a hundred times. A thousand.

He looked so casual, so easy, standing there. But she knew only too well the dangerous edge which lay, barely concealed, beneath the surface. The one that judged her and made her feel lacking.

'You changed crews,' he stated simply. Evenly. That low voice doing things to her insides even now. Even under the cloud she could feel hanging above her, pressing in on her. 'Even before Albert returned to Heathston.'

'The schedule suited me better,' she lied.

She should have known better. Linc quirked one eyebrow upwards, though there was no amusement in it.

'Let us be honest, shall we? You wanted to avoid me.'

'No… I…okay, yes.' Her eyes slipped away from his in shame. 'I did. But can you blame me? After what that tabloid story said about you?'

'This is your apology?' He arched his eyebrows even as the corners of his mouth quirked up.

Remorse flooded instantly through her.

'You're right. I'm sorry. My sister had no right to sell such a story to a paper. It was filled with lies and vitriol—'

'I don't care about your sister, Piper,' he cut her off easily. 'And I certainly don't expect you to have to apologise for the choices *she* made. If anything, she couldn't have sold any story had Sara not alerted her to the fact that you and I were together. So let us not waste our time with any pointless blame game, shall we?'

She frowned at him.

'You understand that Sara was just trying to protect you all.' Piper lifted her shoulders defeatedly. The action revealed far too much of how she really felt, but she couldn't stop herself. 'I know how your sister feels about the importance of family.'

'Then it is unfortunate that she chose to go about it in a way that resulted in more negative attention for us all. But that isn't the apology I am looking for, Piper.'

'It isn't?' She eyed him incredulously as dark things began to fill her up inside.

Could it be the hint of possibility?

'I'm talking about an apology from you,' he clarified, as if he could read every one of the questions that had been flying around her brain up until a few minutes ago. 'For simply leaving like that. For not waiting for me.'

It hit her squarely in the chest. She opened her mouth, closed it again, then drew in a breath.

'You're right. The way I left was cowardly but I couldn't bear the idea of hearing you say to my face how disgusted you were...*are* with me. How I'm the reason for a scandal that you all wanted so badly to avoid. I don't think I want to even imagine the things your sister is calling me right now.'

'I can deal with my sister,' Linc told her ominously. 'Just like I told you I could do that night.'

She wasn't sure it made her feel any better. It was all she could do not to let her shoulders sag suddenly, in defeat. And still that steady gaze held hers, threading through and making her feel hot yet unsettled, all at the same time.

'Why are you here, Piper?'

And this was it. She could bottle it, or she could do what she came here to do.

'I came to talk to you,' she told him simply. 'To ask you a question.'

'Fire away,' he invited.

Reaching into her pocket, she retrieved the letter but, though she held it out towards him, he made no move to take it. Clearly, he was expecting her to talk instead.

'Did you send me a job offer to join you at Stoneywell air ambulance when it's up and running next month?'

And she found she was actually holding her breath, waiting for him to answer.

'I did not.'

It took her a moment to realise that the crashing sound was only in her head.

She should have realised that it had only been her imagination that Linc would still want her. Miss her.

Regret sliced through her.

'Of course you didn't,' she stumbled on, wishing she were anywhere but here, making an even bigger spectacle of herself.

But at least she knew now. She could put that ghost to rest.

'I should… I'll go now.'

'But I knew it about it,' he announced, halting her in her retreat. 'And you aren't asking the right question.'

'The right question?'

He pushed himself off the motorbike and sauntered, too casually, towards her. She could only watch, paralysed. Her throat feeling suddenly parched.

'How does a letter like that get sent out without board approval? Without every member of the board knowing about it?'

Hope jolted in her chest. Kickstarting like an old engine with a faltering battery, but starting all the same.

'How does a job offer like that get sent out without board approval?' she rasped.

'It doesn't.' Linc shrugged.

The silence was almost crushing as it wound around Piper's brain.

'It doesn't? So, you knew? And your brother knew? And...'

'And Sara knew. She sends her apologies, by the way. Grudging and sheepish though they may be, she has finally accepted that her meddling caused this latest debacle.'

'I can't see your sister apologising for anything.' Piper shook her head. 'If anyone knows her own mind, it's Lady Sara—'

'Sara is acutely aware that we all have our secrets,' Linc cut her off, and there was something in the way he said it that made Piper stop. 'She just forgot that salient fact for a while. Call it the noise of her impending nuptials, but she is far more herself now it's all over. She will tell you that in person, if and when you decide you're ready to meet her again.'

'Right.' Piper pursed her lips, not sure she could quite believe that. 'Nevertheless, I know you don't want to hear it again, but I really am sorry about what my sister did.'

'You should have stuck around to tell me that at the time.'

'I was going to,' she admitted, before she could

censure herself. Another detail she hadn't intended to just blurt out.

But the intent look that overtook his angular features stole any other words from her mouth.

'Were you, Piper? You didn't leave the moment I walked out of the door to the wedding?'

'Of course not,' she cried, though perhaps she should have, had she been a more honourable woman. 'I wanted to stay and talk to you. But then the newspapers came out the next morning, and my sister's story splashed all over them…'

'I would hardly call a half-story buried in a middle page *splashed all over them.*'

'No.' She flicked her tongue out over her suddenly dry lips. 'Right. But still, I was ashamed. I didn't think you'd believe I had nothing to do with the piece.'

'Is that really how little you think of me?' he challenged her, a dark frown clouding his maddening, beautiful face.

Something—she didn't care to name what it was—sloshed around inside her.

Had she really thought he wouldn't even hear her out? Or was that just the excuse she'd told herself? The only thing that helped her to push away from her true feelings—the fact that she was in love with Linc.

After all, the only reason she had even been at the wedding rehearsal dinner had been to play at being his fake girlfriend because settling down was the last thing Linc wanted to do.

'I was supposed to be there to make people think you were ready to settle down and return to Oakenfeld. The idea was to get the board members on side. I knew that story could only hurt and there would be no coming back from it.'

'Do you really think Raf and I didn't have a back-up plan?' Linc stepped forward abruptly.

Before she could react, or step back, his palm was cupping her cheek, and moving away wasn't an option. If the entire world had just rocked on its foundations, she wouldn't have been more shocked.

'Linc...'

'You were there because I wanted you there.' His husky voice scraped over her. 'I wanted them to meet you, whatever excuses I may have told you—told myself—at the beginning.'

'You don't mean that,' she managed, but she wasn't sure how.

'I know what I mean, Legs.'

It wasn't just his words that swirled within her chest, making her feel...lighter, and more hopeful, than she thought she'd felt in a long time— perhaps ever. No, more than what he was saying, it was the way that he was looking at her. The intensity of the expression in his gunmetal-grey eyes.

The same expression he'd worn that last night they'd shared, when he'd lifted himself wordlessly above her in bed, their gazes locked as though nothing could tear them apart, and then he'd buried himself so deep inside her that she hadn't known where she'd ended and he'd begun.

Her heart slammed into her chest wall as every fibre of her screamed out to listen. To stop being so hell-bent on protecting herself that she turned her back on something this incredible.

But it wasn't that easy.

'You can't,' she rasped out, finally finding the strength to step back. Away.

But the space didn't make Piper feel better. It just left her feeling empty. Bereft.

'Why can't I?'

And he actually sounded…amused. But how could that be right?

'We're from two entirely different worlds. It wouldn't work. *We* wouldn't work.'

'We're from the same world, you and I.'

'Hardly.' She snorted. 'You're the son of a duke, and I'm the daughter of a woman who was once accused of killing her husband. No matter how false it is, it's one of those things that I don't think will ever go away. You said it yourself.'

'Then we'll find a way to turn it around to our advantage.'

'You can't. Your family don't need the scandal. You told me that, too.'

'My family can handle it. Or *would have* had it been necessary. As it was, the couple of journalists who visited Oakenfeld looking to follow up on your sister's story ended up digging up the fact that you and I used to serve together.'

'Oh.'

'Indeed.' Linc pulled a grim expression. 'They started talking about us as war heroes, which made the board prick up its collective ears. Apparently, they'd never considered using me in that way to enhance the Oakenfeld name.'

'I see,' she managed, not sure whether she really saw at all.

'But even if they hadn't felt that way, it would have been a sorry state if standing up for an abuse survivor like your mother—like you—brought my family scandal,' Linc growled. 'And if it had done, it wouldn't matter because it's the right thing to do.'

'Actually, I spoke to my mother after that newspaper story came out.' Piper almost giggled at the shock of what she was about to say. 'She told me that she was tired of hiding away. Sick of still feeling like she was my father's victim after all these years.'

'Is that so?' Linc arched an eyebrow.

'She said it was almost a relief that my sister had finally done something. That she'd been waiting for some kind of attack all these years and now it had finally come, but no one who knows her seems to care. Some don't even realise it's our family, and those who do have told her how brave and inspirational they think she is.'

'So your mother is happy?' Linc pressed. 'I ask because there's one of the old estate keeper's cottages available, which Sara said she would be more than happy to renovate for your mother and brother. Her way of trying to prove she's sorry.'

'That's…surprisingly sweet of her,' Piper managed. 'Thank you. But my mother is happy where she is. She feels she has people around her who genuinely care for her, and for my brother. She told me that if the story has done anything, it has shown her the kind of good people her friends are—and that she hoped I have the same.'

'So your sister's plan has backfired on all fronts,' Linc mused.

Piper nodded jerkily.

'So it would seem.'

'Yet, even if it hadn't, I would have still been there for you, Piper. I would have stood side by side with you, because I care about you.'

'You care about me.' She heard the torture in her own voice, but that couldn't be helped.

She wanted to hear more. *Needed to.*

'I…care for you, too, Linc.'

Except that wasn't the word she meant to use. Not at all.

'Linc…'

'As for our different backgrounds, which you seem so hung up about, it doesn't matter. You and

I are more alike than you seem to want to admit; we both chose an army life because we thought we could make a difference. We each chose Helimed for the same reason. We're more right for each other than anyone else I know—our different backgrounds don't change that fact.'

'I know,' she muttered, not sure what else to say.

'I hope you do.'

Without warning, he smoothly closed the remainder of the gap between them again. Piper held her breath, waiting for him to reach his palm out to her cheek as before but he didn't. Instead, she found her own hands had crept up and were lying on his chest, though she didn't recall moving.

Clearly her body knew things her head was still denying.

'I love you, Piper Green,' he told her soberly. 'I think I've loved you from the first moment I met you.'

'That was lust,' she croaked, but he shook his head.

'It was love. You were strong, and fearless, and I loved your dry sense of humour from the get-go. Though I'm not denying there was a healthy dose of lust in there, too. Denying it these past few years hasn't helped.'

'You're mistaken,' Piper whispered. But it was crazy how badly she wanted to believe him. 'It was just some silly attraction fuelled by that interrupted kiss. If we'd slept together that night, then it would have all fizzled away years ago and last week would never have happened.'

'You and I both know that's a lie. Nothing would have fizzled away, no matter how many times we slept with each other. Though we weren't the same people back then that we are now. We each had our pasts to deal with, and we needed to come to terms with that in our own time.'

And, for some reason, it was that that made Piper smile the most.

'You're saying we were too immature back then, *Patch*?'

'I would never say that out loud,' he replied dryly.

'I love you, Linc.'

The words were out before she could stop them. But then she repeated them because it felt better than she could ever have imagined to finally be able to admit it. To him, to herself, out loud.

'I love you, too,' he growled, cupping her face in his hands. 'You make me a better man. The man I think I always thought I couldn't be. You make me want the life I have tried to shun, because, with you at my side, I know I can still make a difference.'

He lowered his mouth to hers and finally, *finally*, as he kissed her for what felt like entire, glorious lifetimes, they found their way back to each other.

And when they surfaced at last, with Piper clinging to her lord as they stared at each other in wonder, he reached out and took something from the rucksack at his feet.

'Marry me, Piper.'

She wasn't sure she kept breathing.

For a long moment, she gazed at the stunning ring that seemed to wink at her from its antique box.

'You had that in your bag?'

'I was coming on my way to see you tonight, when I spotted your car hiding over in that corner.'

It took everything she had to try to think straight.

'It's too soon…your family,' she murmured. 'We should wait to see if everything dies down for your brother.'

'Raf can handle himself,' Linc growled. 'He told me so himself. As for waiting, you and I have waited for years.'

It was as if he was echoing the thoughts in her head.

'I want you now, Piper. As my wife, my partner, the mother of my children.'

'I want that too,' she breathed.

'Then marry me.'

'Yes.' She nodded. 'Yes, of course I'll marry you.'

And she watched wordlessly as he slipped the magnificent ring out of the box and onto her finger.

'We can have it resized if it doesn't fit.'

'It fits perfectly,' Piper whispered. 'Like it was meant to be. It's stunning.'

'It's a three-and-a-half-carat marquise-cut diamond that belonged to my great-grandmother. Now it's yours.'

'And now you're mine.' She laughed, as a sort of frothy, fizzy happiness seemed to bubble up inside her, filling her with joy.

It was a revelation. It made her feel as if she was finally home.

* * * * *

If you enjoyed this story, check out these other great reads from Charlotte Hawkes

Forbidden Nights with the Surgeon
Shock Baby for the Doctor
Tempted by Her Convenient Husband
Reunited with His Long-Lost Nurse

All available now!